Endless

K.M. Baker

Content Warning

Please do not skip this page.

There are **STRONG** mentions of self-harm, suicide, and bullying beyond this page. If you are someone who struggles with mental health in any way, please take these content warnings **VERY** seriously!

This is a dark Paranormal Romance. It contains explicit 18+ content that I do not condone outside of a fictional world. Lena struggles, heavily, with self-harm and thoughts of suicide. It is described in depth and may be triggering. There is heavy on page bullying and characters encouraging Lena to self-harm throughout this entire book.

If you feel like there is something that should be added to the below list, please do not hesitate to reach out to me via email at kmbakerauthor@gmail.com

Your mental health matters. You matter.
If you are struggling, help is available.

 K.M. BAKER

Suicide and crisis hotline: Call or Text 988

Triggers:

Adult Language, Anal, Anxiety, Blood, Breath Play, Bullying (Not by MCs), Cheating (Not by MCs), Cutting, Death, Degradation, Depression, Dub-Con, Emotional Abuse, Extreme Verbal Bullying (Not MCs), Grief, Masturbation, Mention of Drugs, Drug Overdose (Not MCs), Mention of Infertility (very small), Public Sex, Self-Harm (on page), Stalking, Suicide, Trauma, Verbal Abuse (Not by MCs), Voyeurism

For anyone who's ever been drawn to death.

Your life matters. You matter.

Playlist

Prologue

Lena

This is what rock bottom feels like. I just know it. I can't stop the tears from freely flowing as I stare off into space and wonder how the fuck I got to this point. I've never felt so alone. I thought this feeling would end after high school, but somehow, it's only gotten worse. From my seated position, I glance down at my wrists and watch as the blood flows from the cuts I just inflicted on myself.

"I think it will be easier for everyone if you go off to your new college without having any connections to Cherry Hill, me included."

That's what my best friend, Dani, told me earlier today while surrounded by a crowd of people. She didn't even have the decency to talk to me about it in private, where we could hash things out and get to what the real problem was. At the ripe age of nineteen, the only person I thought I could depend on proved otherwise.

We never had any issues with our friendship until she started dating Ross. He was one of several people who openly bullied me in high school and she knew this but still tried to convince me that he changed. She insisted that once he graduated, he grew up. I tried to tell her that people like him don't change. They only get better at disguising who they really are. They get better at manipulating others into believing their lies.

Still, she continued to make excuses for his behavior. I didn't want to hear any of them. None of his excuses will change the way he treated me and the things I had to endure.

Everything around me starts to feel colder. I don't think the temperature in the house changed. Another glance down at my wrists reveals large puddles on my bathroom floor. This would have been cleaner if I did it in the bathtub. Whoever finds me is going to have the burden of cleaning up the mess I leave behind. I hope it's not my mom. She always makes everything about herself. I'm sure she will bust out the waterworks and tell the world all about how she had to find her daughter in a puddle of blood. How it stained her perfect marble floors.

I expected Dani to understand where I was coming from. I don't know how she thinks being in a relationship with some-one as cruel as Ross is okay. He wasn't the only one to bully me, but he was the worst of the group. When I was sixteen, he approached me in the lunchroom and cut my ponytail off. My fucking hair. He cut it off and then swung it around, laughing about it with the rest of his fucked-up group of friends.

I hardly consider cutting off someone's hair a joke. Even now, after three years, it only falls to my shoulders. I keep it short on purpose. That group of assholes called me names for the rest of the school year because of him.

I glance down to let my eyes roam over the scars from the cuts I inflicted that day. Two of them on each of my arms, just below the inside of my elbow. I should have cut deeper. Maybe if I did, I could have avoided the way I'm feeling right now.

Dani decided our friendship was no longer something she wished to pursue. It was too hard for her to try and balance her relationship with Ross and her friendship with me. She was tired of being in the middle of the two of us and ultimately chose him. She loves him, so she left me behind.

I'm so confused, and my mind is running in circles. When did things change? When did she feel like she couldn't talk to me anymore? Why was it so easy for her to end our friendship without a second thought? Do I really mean that little to her?

She was the only shoulder I had to cry on throughout high school. She tried her best to protect me, even though it wasn't always something she could do. I was a pariah, and the bullying was constant.

For some unknown reason, I was a target from the time we hit puberty. I never did anything to stand out, and I think that's why they honed in on me. I was always the quiet, weird girl who was always sitting in the corner reading a book or keeping to herself. People are threatened by what they don't know or understand. Nobody knew or understood me. They still don't. Outside of Dani, that is. Well, was.

It might seem strange to have such a drastic reaction to a friendship ending. This friendship was the only thing that lifted me up and saved me from some of my darkest times. She was there for me to lean on when my grandma passed and told me I'd never be alone. *Lie.*

My grandma was my person, and Dani filled those shoes for a while. Not anymore. There is nobody here to help me pick up the pieces this time, certainly not my shitty parents. I'm left in the dark with no prospect of finding the light.

My family will never understand. I've struggled with my mental health my entire life. They tried to tell me, 'It's a phase; you'll grow out of it.' My mother insisted high school is hard for everyone, and once I got into the real world, it would all change. They firmly believed I just needed to get a better handle on how to express my emotions. My mother clearly has no idea how mental health works.

I know exactly how I want to express my emotions. The blade sitting on the floor next to my bloody arms seems like a pretty good fucking way. It's the only way I know to express anything anymore.

My thoughts always win. *Just cut a little deeper. It's not enough. This one needs to go further, so maybe I'll actually feel something besides the numbness that currently spreads through my heart.* I glide the razorblade against my skin again, and the trail of red instantly begins to flow from it. Blood oozes onto the floor to meet the puddle from the previous cuts.

The edges of my vision begin to darken, and I notice I no longer have feeling in my fingers or toes. I should get up, but I can't move. Everything around me has a haze to it now. It's almost as though I am looking at it from the outside. *Finally*, I think, and I welcome the feeling.

A shadow figure in the hallway outside the bathroom catches my attention. Black tendrils of smoke spiral along the carpet. I try to lift my head higher to get a better look at what they're connected to, but I'm too weak. I watch with astonishment as the smoke-like tendrils inch toward me.

I think I might have finally done it this time. I've let the numbness consume my body, and a tear slips from the corner of one of my deep brown eyes. This is the part where I get to be free from it all, right? My eyes flicker closed as the shadows stop directly beside me.

I'm shaken awake violently by my mother screaming in my face. "LENA! What did you do? How could you do this to yourself? Look at this mess."

My mouth falls open to answer her, but nothing comes out. I want to tell her to leave me be. Let me move on from this cruel world the way I want to. Just let me have my moment, grieve me, and get on with your life. That's what I want more than anything. Just let me die.

My eyes flutter closed as I tune her out, and the darkness takes me under. When they open again, I'm in a bed covered from the waist down with a dark, scratchy blanket. My arms lie by my sides, palms up, with bandages covering them from my elbows to my wrists.

I take a deep breath, realizing my mother found me in time. I can't even kill myself properly. The one time she showed up to save me was when I didn't want to be saved. Fucking figures.

Chapter 1

Lena - 2 years later

College is supposed to be easy and fun. The last years of our dying youth, but this doesn't feel fun. In fact, it's been a long time since I was able to feel anything besides empty. The last two years have been riddled with one disappointment after another. Just like the rest of my fucking life.

After my mother very rudely interrupted my impending death on the bathroom floor of her perfect home, she sent me to the hospital to recover. I was barely there for a week. When I got home, I found all of my things packed up. She was ready to send me off to college without a single word.

There was no discussion, no talks of therapy, or questions as to why I did what I did. She simply found me bleeding out on her marble floors, sent me away long enough for the cuts to start healing, and moved on to pretend as though nothing happened. Mental illness does not exist to my parents. Me missing college makes her and my father look weak. We can't have that.

The only plus side of being here is not being in that house with them. My mother checks in every few days to make sure I'm keeping up with my studies, but neither she nor my father ever asks me how I'm doing or brings up trying to kill myself.

Not the attempt two years ago or any of the others before that. They just wear their rose-colored glasses and pretend their daughter isn't fucked in the head.

I close my eyes and remember the dark shadowy figure that filled my vision before the darkness consumed me. Something about seeing the partial figure tells me I was close that time. I was only a few seconds away from finding relief from this fucked up world.

Instead, I'm here at this shitty college with a shitty boyfriend and fake-ass friends, pretending I'm happy. I'm good at plastering a fake smile on my face to pretend everything is fine on the outside. People don't want to know about your struggles. Nobody wants to be there for you. I learned that the hard way the day Dani decided Ross meant more than our friendship.

The best part about the entire situation with her was the two of them broke up less than six months later. She tried to call and text me to reconnect, but I simply told her, 'Sorry, Dani, it's better for everyone if I don't have any connections to Cherry Hill.' I threw the same words she uttered to me right back in her face, and I don't feel bad about it. Even if I could find it in me to forgive her, things would never be the same after how she treated me.

Dani choosing to end our friendship set off a series of events that screamed, 'Let's fuck over Lena in every way possible.' I've done my best to try to keep my head held high through every single one of them, but I don't think I can do it anymore.

Mentally, I'm right on the precipice of where I was when I slit my wrists on the bathroom floor.

My phone pings, and I glance down to see a video text from a phone number I don't recognize. Scratch that—messages—from multiple numbers I don't recognize begin pouring in.

> Unknown: I didn't realize how much of a dirty whore you are. The whole campus knows now, though.

> Unknown: Fuck, I'd love to see you ride my cock like that.

> Unknown: So, you like to choke on dick?

> Unknown: I always knew you were a slut.

I can't read any more. What the fuck are they talking about? With shaky fingers, I click on the video, and what I see shocks me to my core. It's me, face down, ass up, being railed from behind as Carson slaps my ass and calls me a needy bitch.

My cheeks redden from embarrassment, and my chest tightens. I take quick breaths, trying to calm myself before dropping my phone and staring at the wall of our apartments living room. The video continues playing, and I hear myself tell him to fuck me harder. Oh my God, this can't be happening.

I don't know what else to do besides pick up the phone and watch the rest of the video, which I'm assuming hundreds of others are also watching at this exact moment. Carson pushes down on the back of my neck, holding me in place with one hand, and slaps my ass with the other.

A fucking sex tape, really? It couldn't be just an innocent, grainy five-second clip, either. This is clear as day, full porn production, with my spread open pussy on display for everyone to see multiple times. The world feels like it's caving in on me. I just want to be invisible.

I'm not ashamed of the way I like to get fucked. I like it dirty, and there is absolutely nothing wrong with that. What I'm struggling with is the teasing that will come from this. People are cruel. They can't resist the urge to be shitty humans, and this is a huge opportunity for them. I already know I will be the focus of everyone's interests for the next who the hell knows how long. Just the thought makes me cringe.

I was doing so well. I haven't let myself touch a blade in two years, but this right here is too much. The incessant comments that I know will stem from this TWENTY-MINUTE video push me over the edge.

Subconsciously, I stand up like a zombie and walk toward the bathroom. Each step feels feather-light. My mind leads me, and my body blindly follows. *He let everyone see me naked and vulnerable. I thought what we had was special. I'm nothing. I'm not worth anything to anyone.* The dark thoughts consume me again.

I blink and stare at myself in the mirror, studying my reflection. I don't know how I got here. I'm sure I walked the rest of the way, but I don't remember doing it. My mind operated on autopilot.

I look down at my shaky hands. I need to get my shit together. I told myself this wouldn't happen again. I lift my hand in front of my face and stare at my trembling fingers before glancing back at the familiar vacant shadow of my eyes in the mirror. The bright brown hue they used to carry has already begun to fade again. Dull and empty. Aching and in pain. There's always so much pain. There's always another door being slammed in my face or another person proving they aren't who they seem. The numbness. It's all endless.

I grip the edge of the sink, willing tears to fall, but they don't. If I could just cry, maybe I could let it all out and move on. I glance over my shoulder, and my eyes land on the razor in the corner. I'm fixated on it. I can't force myself to move. I should get out of this bathroom. The faint sound of a door opening and closing makes me blink, bringing back some awareness.

Put it on. Put the mask back on. Don't let anyone know you're struggling. Don't let them see your weaknesses. I step over to the toilet with nothing in it to flush it before standing in front of the sink and washing my hands. I don't need to wash them, but I do anyway. It's the perfect cover for me being in here.

"Lena?" Carson calls out as he heads toward our bathroom. We've had this apartment together since the start of the school year. The year that was supposed to be fun and carefree, yet here I am, heading back into the downward spiral.

"In here!" I call out.

My hands still tremble as I rinse off the rest of the soap. *Put the mask back on, Lena.* I tell myself as I grab the decorative towel off the hanger to dry my hands.

"Hey, I was wondering where you were." He steps into me and plants a kiss on my cheek.

He let everyone see the look on your face when you come. I push the thought to the back of my mind.

"Just going to the bathroom. Why are you home so early? Did you skip your afternoon class?"

"The professor canceled. Something about her kid. We got the afternoon off, so I figured I would come home to see my pretty girl."

My broken eyes meet his. He knows I know. I can't help but notice the way he stares at me longer than usual.

"Do you want to go get lunch somewhere off campus?" he says while wrapping his hand around my waist.

I have to fight every urge in me to not flinch away. *Don't give him a reason to think you aren't okay. Don't think about the razor in the corner that's calling out to you.* I place my hand flat on his chest to glance up at him and lie.

"I'm sorry I can't today. I have a few errands to run around town." I don't have errands to run but he can't call me out on the lie without openly admitting what he did.

I could meet up with Lexi, but I don't want to talk about this with anyone yet. Lexi is my best friend. At least to the world, that's who she is. To me, she is just the first person who was nice to me on campus. I've managed to open myself up to her just a smidge more than usual, but she doesn't really know me. Nobody does. Nobody has since Dani. I won't let myself go through something like that ever again.

My phone makes a noise, and I do my best not to look down at it.

Even Carson, my boyfriend for nearly a year, doesn't know me. He only sees the Lena I want him to. The real me is dark, damaged, and unlovable. Everyone thinks he is someone I should covet. 'He's a keeper. You're thriving with him. You two make such a cute couple. Imagine what your children will look like.' That's what they all say.

Carson is only a keeper because he is the perfect cover. My parents think I'm happy. The friends I entertain think he balances me out. It'll always be fake because nobody like him would ever understand who I really am.

Maybe I don't know him either. I didn't even know he was recording us having sex. How many other videos does he have? I need to get out of here and find somewhere quiet to pull myself together.

"Dinner at Mount Chellos tonight?" Carson says to me, reminding me that I'm still in the room with him.

I step away from his side and peer up to find him looking down at me with the same weary glance he's had since coming home. More texts come through my phone. How the fuck did all of these people even get my phone number? I don't want to go to dinner. I don't want to be around him right now while I try to process this. He won't let up until I agree to something.

"I don't know if I'm in the mood for anything that fancy," I admit.

"Lena, your phone has been going off since I walked into the apartment. I know you saw the video." My jaw clenches, and I avert my eyes from him, refusing to admit that he's right. "Let me make it up to you," he says, trying to stroke my cheek.

"It's fine, really." *It's not fine,* I think.

"You're not upset with me?" he asks, wrapping his hand around my waist and pulling me into him.

"No, Carson. I don't want to talk about it right now either. I'm on edge. You know I need to make sure my anxiety doesn't get the best of me. It's better if I just forget about it."

"I didn't know she was going to send it out to everyone. She's been trying to get me to break up with you. She won't accept that I want you."

She? Who the fuck is she? Is he cheating on me now, too? I should have seen this coming. I try my best to keep my breathing even and my face emotionless. I need to get out of here.

I grab my keys off of the holder near the door and walk back over to him to give him a chaste peck on the lips. "I'll be back in a little bit. We can go somewhere close for dinner."

"Okay. If that's what you want. I just want to make it up to you."

"There's nothing to make up. It's fine."

With that, I open the door and walk to my car. I already know where I'm going. I can't be in that apartment with him. If there was hell, this would be it. It's almost a sick joke that nobody in my life is real or genuine. They're all just as fake as I am when I tell them I'm okay. How the fuck am I supposed to go on like this? Something has to give at some point, right?

Chapter 2
Kellan

She seems on edge today, like something transpired between her and that shitty boyfriend she spends her time with. I'm not entirely sure why she continues to put up with him. He doesn't benefit her in any way. It's a curious thing, really.

I've watched her closely from a distance for some time now. Distance is all I'm afforded because no matter how much I want her, I can't have her.

My job is simple, wait for the right time and lead them down their path. Do not intervene. I'd never been tempted to intervene until I laid eyes on this raven-haired beauty. She's such a strange, alluring creature.

The Angel of Death, Grim Reaper, Santa Muerte, and Azarel are just a few of the names I go by. I haven't had the luxury of someone calling me by my true name in a long time. If I had the choice, people would just call me Kellan. All of my aliases seem so... final.

In a way, everything I do is final. I spend the entirety of my existence ensuring those who cross my path end up on their correct one. Aside from the date, time of their death and name, I know nothing about them. I don't need to know anything else.

I am only a neutral bystander who leads and watches while they carry out their purpose in my realm.

Not everyone ends up with me. Most find their way automatically to either Heaven or Hell based on how they live their human lives. The ones I am tasked to lead are those who either have unfinished business or need to be tested. These souls come to my realm to find their purpose.

I never introduce myself to them. When souls see me, they already know who I am—the personification of death. I'm not to make any sort of connection with those whose paths cross mine. That's not one of my tasks because it could potentially interfere with their purpose. That is the greatest rule: Do not interfere with a soul's purpose.

The only time I'm afforded glimpses of the souls I am to lead, outside my usual job, is if they evade me. Not everything is cut and dry when I am involved. Although nobody ever completely outruns death, sometimes they do not end up in my immediate grasp. The dates and times of their deaths change, usually due to the actions of others. They are temporarily saved from their walk with me. If this happens and I've revealed myself without claiming their soul, a tether forms between us. These tethers become invisible strings that link us together. I have full access to everything they do in their human lives until we ultimately meet again.

If I wanted to, I could watch them from the shadows of the human world until their true time of death arises. I've never wanted to. Human life is not something I particularly care about. My job is to worry about the souls in my realm. It's a purgatory of sorts. Each soul that enters my dominion has an allotted amount of time to prove themselves in one way or another. I don't decide the time it will take or how it is done. That's up to the Others.

Once they find their purpose, the angel or demon will appear to take them beyond. Where souls end up after they leave my realm is a direct result of their time spent here. I don't know where that is, nor do I care. I've never really cared what happens to these souls once they move on from me. I only watch as needed to ensure they stay on their path.

Humans have never meant anything to me; Lena became my exception. The moment my eyes landed on her, I knew she was going to be different than all of the others. I've seen so many throughout my existence, but none have piqued my interest in the way she does. There is pain in her shimmering brown eyes, but she is able to mask it with a blank facade that lesser beings would be oblivious to.

Time works differently for me. There is no start or finish. Two human years ago, I saw her for the first time, broken and bloody on her bathroom floor, and I was instantly enchanted. It only took one glance at her for the image of her high cheekbones and full lips to be ingrained in my memory for all of eternity. Aside from the few freckles sprinkled around her button nose, her porcelain skin is clear as day. She is a striking beauty.

On the outside, she may appear to be more of the girl next door type, but she is deeply tortured. She has mastered her fake smile for the rest of the world, but as I mentioned, I am privy to seeing things in people that mere humans are not.

The darkness in her soul speaks to me on a level that I don't understand, even after two years. She is broken, beautiful, and desperately trying to seek out something she will likely never find in her lifetime.

This one broken soul craves nothing except for the peace of the end. She has no clue that Death has been watching her. Today, she looks sadder than usual as she strolls from her apartment building to her old rundown car. It's almost as though she doesn't want anyone to see where she's going. Obviously, I'm going to follow her to find out what she's up to. My perfect little pet, who captivates all of my attention.

She won't see me. Nobody sees me in my true shadow form unless I will them to. I've considered revealing myself to her in my human form just so I can have some sort of interaction with her but keeping a distance will be too hard for me once I do.

When people think of the personification of death, they automatically assume I resemble what they read about in their books or what they see on their screens—a skeleton figure in a long black robe wielding a scythe. While I suppose my magic grants me the option to appear like that, the scythe is more of a hassle than it's worth to carry around. My true form is much more complex.

The best way to describe my most authentic self is a firm cloud of smoke. A conundrum, I know, but as free as the smoke flows, it also has the ability to be solid. I can bend the shadows at my will, as they are extensions of myself. The dark tendrils often dance at my feet. When in my natural state, I keep myself cloaked in a long, hooded robe. I guess humans have at least that description of me correct.

My human form is what most consider to be attractive. I have short black hair and a strong jawline. A range of different tattoos cover most of my upper body. My arms house different designs, such as black roses and smoky tendrils. I'm fit but not overly muscular. My green hooded eyes are my most striking feature. I never miss the way the humans stare into them, wishing they could see further into my being to learn more about who I am. Humans have always been curious creatures, looking to find deeper connections in one another.

My attention falls back to my pet as she starts her car and pulls off in the opposite direction. I already know where she's going. It's where she always goes when she's upset, but even if she doesn't go there, I will always find her. We have been connected since the first time we saw one another.

I pop over to the cemetery and wait for her to arrive. There is a bench that she likes to sit on, so I hide in the tree line near it. She enjoys coming here to look out on the one thing she craves the most: death.

She's addicted to finding the release of the end. I wonder if that's why she feels the need to harm herself. Maybe the closer to death she is, the more calm she feels.

Sometimes, she tries talking to the dead as if they can hear her. These people have all moved on to the great beyond. The only thing out here that hears her is me.

Her car finally comes into view, and she parks it in her usual spot. She steps out, and the light hits her hair in the most perfect way, causing it to shine as it blows in the faint breeze. She is wearing a pair of black leggings and a long-sleeve crew-neck sweater today. The fall weather compliments her well.

She strides over to her bench and sits down, pulling her knees to her chest and resting her cheek on them. After a few minutes, she sighs loudly and lifts her head to look at the graves in front of her. The empty look in her eyes tells me something major happened.

"How the hell am I supposed to show my face in class tomorrow after the entire campus saw me getting fucked by my boyfriend?" she confesses to the quiet space around her.

He did what? A strange feeling courses through me. Is this anger? No, surely not. I've never felt angry before.

"So many text messages from people on campus. They saw everything," she whispers, defeated.

Yes. This must be anger. Knowing so many people saw her in such a vulnerable position unwillingly causes fury to consume me. I clench my fists, and my shadow tendrils fill the air next to me. My body morphs into a mixture of my human and shadow form as I struggle to control my emotions.

"I really thought I had something decent going here. People were friendly enough. Sure, I've dealt with a few things, but overall, it wasn't anything extreme. I was able to resist the call of the blades." She sighs again, shaking her head as tears well up in her gorgeous eyes. I want to be there to wipe them away for her.

"It's all going to change now. The bullying is going to start again. I don't know if I'm strong enough to handle it. I've been trying so hard to pretend I'm okay. Nobody will even see it coming this time, but I know it's inevitable. They're going to push me too hard, and I'm going to end up bloody on the bathroom floor again." She wipes her tears with her sleeve.

A tendril reaches out from me as if my very being aches to comfort her before I remember I'm not supposed to show myself to her. If I do, I might change things, and I don't want to risk that. I take a step backward into the shadows, trying my best to keep my anger at bay. I force myself to calm down and morph back into my human form. I'm not used to feeling emotions, but my pet always has a way of surprising me.

She continues confessing everything to the dead. "He said something about some other girl being the one to send it out to campus. I don't even know why he had that kind of video of the two of us. Add in the fact that some girl had access to his phone. It's all just one fucked up mess. Story of my life. I guess that's why I would rather be like you. It's so peaceful. I crave that."

I know you do, my pet. You can't give in and succumb to the peace just yet. That would mean our time together would end. I think to myself. We've been on a ticking clock since the moment I first laid eyes on her. If it were up to me, I would keep her forever. I've never wanted to keep a soul as much as I want to keep hers. That's just not realistic.

"I would have cut myself again if he didn't come home when he did. I was so close to grabbing the razor and just letting the relief wash over me. I'm trapped with all of those feelings, and tomorrow, they are going to be so much worse. I should go back to the apartment and give myself the relief I crave. I can't, though. If I go there, Carson will probably be up my ass trying to apologize," she cries out in frustration.

I watch for a while longer before I find myself being pulled away to complete a task. I don't want to leave her here like this. I want to be able to comfort her or, at the very least, watch to make sure she's okay, but there are souls that need tending to. I have a job to do. I take one last glance at her teary eyes and reluctantly vanish to perform my duties.

Chapter 3

Lena

The sun starts to set over the graveyard, and I know I should go back to my apartment, but I don't want to. I don't think I have the strength to pretend everything is okay right now. I just want things to end, but I'm too much of a coward to try and fail again. All I can do is stew in my feelings of worthlessness and despair.

I have class tomorrow morning, and every eye will be on me from the moment my feet land on campus. I wrestle with whether or not I should face Carson at all tonight. It might do him some good to wonder where I am after the shit he pulled. If I go home, he will try to make me forgive him and smother me with some kind of love and affection. The thought of it makes my stomach churn.

I should cut him off completely and move on like any normal female would do when she's been wronged in this capacity. I'll never fully forgive or trust him after this, but the idea of being completely alone again scares me. I'm not sure what my mind would be willing to do when I only have my own thoughts to stew in. The darkness that always threatens the corners of my soul will try to pull me back under again. Even if it's a superficial relationship, for now, it's better than everyone thinking I'm alone. That would just be more for them to talk about.

I should figure out how many more videos exist. Fuck. I want to be upset at him, but I don't want to risk hurting him and having a slew of videos leaked on the internet for the world to see. One is bad enough. I need to find out more about the situation before I make any kind of drastic move. I have to let him think he can make it up to me.

The sun has now set, leaving twilight in its wake. I stand from the bench and take one last deep breath before walking to my car. It's chilly but not cold enough for me to get hyperthermia from sleeping in my car. As much as I welcome death, hyperthermia seems like a terrible way to go.

I open the door to the back seat and slide in, shutting it behind me. I grab my bag with miscellaneous clothing and rummage through it. I keep this somewhere in my car at all times. My life experiences have taught me that it's always better to have spare clothing than to be forced to walk around in potentially ruined ones for the entirety of the day. Another lovely lesson from high school. A person can only endure so many days of smelling like spoiled milk before learning from it.

I pull a sweater over my head to add an extra layer of warmth while I sleep. If I get too cold, I can always turn the heat on for a little bit. I grab another shirt, bundle it into a ball to make myself a pillow, and glance down at my bed for the night. How fucking pathetic am I? Being alone with my thoughts makes me want to do something drastic.

Before I know what I'm doing, I slip out of the backseat and find myself behind the wheel. I start the car and drive to the nearest supermarket to obtain the only thing my mind hasn't been able to free itself from since seeing the video.

I park and walk inside, heading straight to the section with all the shaving products. People never question someone purchasing things like this. The men's double-edge razor blades are my go-to. They take the least amount of effort to obtain the desired effect. After grabbing a few other things, I make my way back to the front of the store. Quickly, I pay the cashier and find myself back in my car.

Within a few minutes, I'm parking in my favorite spot at the cemetery again. Nobody bothers me when I'm here, regardless of the time. They know my car and know that I show nothing but respect to the dead.

The dead have always been nicer to me than any living person I've ever encountered. They don't judge or make me feel like my thoughts or feelings are invalid. They simply listen.

I grab the bag with the razor blades and use the light on my phone to walk back over to the bench that has become my refuge since coming to Thorn Grove. It would be a shame to get blood all over my car. After setting my phone down with the light shining up, I pull the razors, gauze package, and tape from the bag and set them next to me on the bench.

I stare at the razors, questioning if I should really open myself up to this again. I know letting myself do this may be a giant step backward, but I need the relief. There are too many thoughts coursing through my head right now to resist the pull. Had Carson not come home earlier when he did, I would have already done this and moved on from the feelings.

Having them built up inside me has only made the urge worse. *I can just make one or two cuts. It won't be a habit again.* I tell myself. I know I'm lying, but I also don't care enough to try to talk myself out of it anymore.

I grab the package of blades, rip it open, and pull one of them out. The light from my phone causes a glare in the metal as I hold it in front of my face. I'm fixated on it for a moment, waiting for my mind to tell me not to do this. This isn't going to make anything better. This isn't going to change the fact that the entire campus saw me getting dicked down. My mind doesn't want me to stop, so I do what my instincts tell me to do.

I push up my sleeves and give into the darkness, letting the overwhelming feeling possess my body. The edge of the blade glides over my skin just enough for a light trail of blood to ooze from its wake. I breathe heavily as I watch the red liquid drip from my wrist and onto the bench.

Chills spread throughout my body, and relief instantly follows. I make another cut next to this one, pushing a little deeper this time. The blood flows a bit more from this wound, but it's still not enough to put me at risk of bleeding out. I don't want to kill myself right now. I just need to feel something familiar.

Dragging this blade across my skin is the first real thing I've felt in almost two years. I've been pretending to be someone I'm not. I've been putting on a fake smile and cultivating fake relationships with people to try and be the person society expects me to be. This right here, this is the real me. This is the raw, uncaring, natural Lena Hill at her best or worst, maybe both.

I drag the sharp edge along my wrist one last time for a third and final cut. The tension in my shoulders recedes, and I can almost breathe normally again. The adrenaline starts to wear off, so I close my eyes and take a deep breath, centering myself. Shame floods through me for a brief moment before I will it away. *I had to do this. I'm not weak. I had to do it so I could deal with the stares tomorrow. Everything is fine. I'm not going to let it get bad again.*

With that last thought, I rip open the gauze, place it over my wrist, and tape it down. I don't want the blood getting onto my clothing. I'll wash and disinfect everything tomorrow. I sigh and walk back to my car with the bloody blade wrapped in another piece of gauze that I placed safely in the package. After tossing the contents on the front seat, I crawl to my makeshift bed in the back and let my restless dreams overtake me.

****

I pry my eyes open and stare at the ceiling momentarily, dreading what is to come from this day. The sun shines brightly into the windows of my car, reminding me that I slept at the cemetery. I sit up to stretch and take a few deep breaths. The will to go on with the day is very minimal right now, but I don't have a choice.

I dig through the bag of my spare clothing and find something comfortable to wear with long sleeves. I can't have the evidence from last night showing for the masses. I've caught some strange looks toward my old scars, but nobody's had the gall to say anything about them. If they saw the fresh cuts, I know for sure they would shame me. They already have enough to gossip about today without me adding to it.

I glance down at my phone and see a few messages from Carson that I don't bother reading. I'm still not ready to talk to him. He's likely wondering where I am, but he can keep wondering. I bet he wasn't thinking about where I was when he was with whatever girl sent out the video of me and him fucking. I'm angry at him today, which is good. Anger is an emotion, right? At least I'm feeling something other than empty.

After putting on a fresh change of clothes, I spray dry shampoo into my hair and throw it up in a ponytail. It's not the best look, but I don't care. I slide into the front seat and freeze for a moment before letting autopilot take over for the drive back to Thorn Grove. The campus comes into sight, and I park in my usual spot before grabbing my backpack from the trunk.

I walk through the quad with my head down and my eyes laser-focused on the ground in front of me. I can't bring myself to look at the crowd of people I stroll through. I can feel their gazes practically burning into my skin. The whispers around me are not as quiet as they think they are.

"Oh my God, did you see the video of her?"

"She is such a slut."

"I can't believe she let her boyfriend film her."

"I thought she was weird before. I guess I was right."

"I can't believe she had the balls to show her face today."

"She knows everyone saw it, right?"

"What if she's the one that sent it out?"

Each one cuts into me like a knife. I wish it was an actual knife instead. I just have to make it through my classes, and I can go back to my apartment to find some relief. During class, there shouldn't be anything I have to overhear. The breaks between them are going to be the biggest issue.

I make it through the first break fairly easily, but the break between my second and third class is much longer. I have to go to the other side of campus, and typically, I stop at the dining hall to grab lunch beforehand. My stomach growls at the thought of food. I haven't eaten anything since breakfast yesterday.

I take a deep breath and will my body toward the dining hall. *I'll just keep my eyes down and ignore the comments. It'll be fine.* Except it's not fine. As soon as I walk in, I make the mistake of glancing around the room, and everyone goes quiet. Everyone is staring at me as I step in front of the cooler full of ready-made sandwiches. I grab a random cold cut, eager to get out of here as fast as possible.

When I turn to walk toward the check-out, a woman steps in front of me with her arms crossed over her chest. I've seen her around campus before. We don't share any classes, but she always hangs around the football team. She's got perfect long blonde hair and always has her makeup firmly in place. She's the exact type of person you would look at and just know she's a mean girl.

"You know, we always wondered why Carson would date someone like you, but it all makes perfect sense now. You're the only slut willing to fulfill his sexual fantasies. I bet you liked it when you found out he was recording you, didn't you?"

I try to step to the side to walk around her, but she steps in front of me again. I don't see how shaming me makes her feel better. I get increasingly annoyed at her continued presence.

"I bet you'd let one of his friends fuck you at the same time and film that too. You would probably let the entire football team run a train on your used-up pussy."

"Get the fuck out of my way," I grit out, making her laugh in my face.

"You're a pathetic excuse of nothing, a waste of space, Lena. Nobody wants anything to do with you now that we've all seen what you're good for. Nothing but a slut who's willing to do anything for someone to fuck her. Carson isn't just fucking you, though. Maybe you should ask him about me."

She laughs again and finally steps to the side, leaving me to stare at her as she walks away. Was she the one who leaked the video? Or is she another woman Carson could be cheating on me with?

My head spins as I approach the cash register to ring myself out. I grab the sandwich I no longer desire to eat and go straight to my car. After the run-in with that cunt in the dining hall, I'm skipping my last class for the day. My professor will just have to get over it. The blades in my car are calling out to me again.

Chapter 4

Kellan

She walks through the crowd, her head bowed as they all comment about her under their breath, things nobody should ever have to endure hearing. It wasn't her fault, yet they make it seem like it is.

She doesn't want to draw any attention to herself, which is ironic considering who she chooses to spend her time with. She could have picked anyone, but she ended up with the quarterback of the football team. It was only a matter of time before he did something to bring this kind of negative attention to her. He can't resist the urge to make everything about himself. His time is growing near. I can feel it.

A familiar but strange, angry feeling eats at me when I think of what he did to her. He is trying to pull her back to the darkest pits of her mind. I have to find a way to make sure she doesn't go there. I'm not ready for our time together to be cut short. He should just let her go. It would all be so much easier if he would spare her the humiliation.

I watch her in my human-like form, disguising myself in the crowd as if I were another one of them. Nobody here will see the true me, not any time soon. I'm not allowed to intentionally show humans my true shadow self unless I am there to transport their soul. It's a stupid rule.

I've never had a desire to linger amongst them for as long as I have been lately. I've found myself spending more and more time in my human form to be near her. She has been slowly shifting something inside me from the moment I first laid eyes on her.

After the video exposed her to the majority of Thorn Grove, I feel more protective of her. It's another feeling I've never previously felt with this fiery level of intensity. It's a problem. I'm not unfamiliar with emotions. I've just never had the need for them until my broken beauty crossed my path. Anything I've felt before her was nothing more than a fleeting moment through time.

She gets through the first part of her day without any major issues. They make comments under their breath, but she avoids gazing at them. She keeps to herself, walking with her eyes glued to the ground.

Just as she gets ready to get her lunch, at the same time she normally does, I feel myself being called away. I pause momentarily before giving her one last glance and shrinking into the shadows to disappear. Stupid work.

I'm away for a good portion of the day, leaving her to fend for herself. If I could shield her from their torment without risking the very purpose of her being, I would. I'm starting to realize I would do just about anything for her, and I haven't even been granted the satisfaction of a simple conversation. She knows nothing about me, but I know as much as I can about her.

By the time I'm able to get near her again, my pet is asleep in her bed. I had to see her, so I let myself into her apartment and I'm currently watching from the shadows. There was a mass casualty event today that took up more of my time than expected. Every time I finished leading one soul, another was calling out for me. On days like today, I consider how helpful it would be to have a partner to assist with the job. My eyes roam back to Lena. What if she could be by my side to help me? I shake the thought from my mind. It's not possible. It would never be allowed. Death doesn't get a partner. Death is meant to be alone, final.

She twitches in her sleep. Maybe she can sense me in her unconscious state. *You're not as alone as you think you are, pet.* Her loser boyfriend is out partying, surely finding another way to cause her pain. I wish I could intervene, but I'm left in the shadows to observe as the only person I've ever developed feelings for feels nothing but pure anguish.

Feelings. They have been slowly growing stronger since the moment I first saw her. I'm not supposed to let things get out of hand like this because it complicates things—like right now. She twitches again, almost as though she is having a bad dream, and all I want to do is pull her into my grasp to coax her into a restful sleep.

I watch the rise and fall of her perfect chest. The blanket has gathered at her waist, and her shirt is plastered to her skin, revealing her hard nipples. They are aching for me to reach out and touch them. A moan leaves her lips, and I stop breathing. I'm frozen in place from the most glorious sound that I've ever heard. She's not having a bad dream at all.

She shifts again, and one of her legs frees itself from the blanket. Another sweet whimper falls from her. It takes everything in me to not step out of the shadowed corner and force her to make more of these sounds. I'm intoxicated by them.

Even with the pull I've felt toward her, I've always tried to give her privacy when she is in the comfort of her home. I pop in to check on her and leave. I've never heard her make these sounds before, mostly because I don't like seeing her with her boyfriend. This is the apartment they share, and he sours my mood. I wish I could end him, but that's not allowed.

I'm glad he wasn't home when I appeared here. I don't want to see him anywhere near her. I haven't seen the video, but when another whimper leaves her lips, I find myself wondering if these are the same noises she made in it.

A familiar bell rings inside my mind, indicating someone is ready for me to help them cross into my realm. I have to go, and for the first time, I consider not leaving. If I leave, I could miss the way her face scrunches up when she makes more of these whimpering noises. I wonder what she is dreaming about. Who is giving her the sweet pleasure as she rests?

Reluctantly, I vanish into the night to appear in front of the person I am here to collect. It is an older woman, and I find myself hoping this moves along swiftly so I can return to my pet.

The wrinkles along the old woman's sagging cheeks tell a story of her life, similar to the crow's feet that spread from her eyes and lines across her forehead. She looks up at me from her hospital bed with nothing but acceptance in her eyes. These ones are the easiest. The ones that seem to have lived a full life.

I step forward and reach out my hand to prompt her to take it, and she does so without a single question. I walk her hand in hand to my realm where she can fulfill her purpose. I don't know what her path will look like. It could be years full of turmoil and challenge or mere moments of joy and acceptance. The old woman looks up at me as I release her hand, giving her a silent nod. She smiles and nods back. With that, I disappear from her sight.

I feel nothing for the old woman. I feel nothing for anyone except for my raven-haired pet. I long to return to her. When I reappear in the shadowy corner of her room that I previously occupied, I am startled by the sight in front of me.

My perfect Lena is spread wide open for me to see. Her feet are planted on the bed with her legs bent at the knee as she uses her fingers to rub at her center. She arches her back off the bed and uses her free hand to grope her breast. I want to reach out and wrap my shadowy tendrils around her throat and ask what she's thinking about. What is making her so needy? Who is on her mind?

Her fingers dip inside her glistening cunt, and I know this is going to change me in the most unexpected yet glorious way. I don't know how much longer I'll be able to continue as a neutral bystander. Am I even neutral at this point? I crave her taste on my tongue. I want to feel the way she writhes beneath me as she arches her back, begging for more, similar to what she is doing now.

I should leave to prevent this feeling from deepening, but now my breathing is heavy, and all I want is to be here with her. I reach down to grip my aching shadow cock. Slowly, I stroke myself, keeping my eyes on her the entire time. I don't want to miss a single second of this moment. It will be burned into my memories so I can play it on a loop for all of eternity.

The way the center of her brow creases as she parts her lips and lets out another moan has my breath catching. She moves her fingers faster in and out of her pussy as her other hand slides down to find her clit. Her eyes squeeze shut as if she inches closer and closer to her orgasm.

I yearn to touch her. I stroke myself faster, picturing what it would be like to sink inside her walls. Her slick pussy would stretch around me so perfectly. One of my shadowy tendrils moves from my corner of the room. It inches closer to where she is positioned on the bed, with a mind of its own at this point. I don't have the willpower to stop it.

"Fuck," she cries out while curling her toes.

The pressure builds inside me, growing nearer and nearer to bursting at the seams. I won't crest that hill without her. The tendril slides up the side of the bed just as another moan falls from her delectable lips.

"Yes!" She screams and pushes herself to climax.

I imagine her tight pussy gripping onto my cock as she rides out her blissful high, and I find mine with her. Come shoots from the tip of my shadow cock, coating my hand just as the tendril wraps itself around one of her wrists. She is still coming down from her orgasmic bliss and doesn't notice; however, I quickly collect myself and retract it.

This was far too much of a risk. If she saw me, it could ruin everything. I try to center my thoughts, but my mind continues to race. She looks so beautiful right now. The deep pink on her cheeks accentuates her normally pale skin. She takes one more deep breath and sits up in the bed. I glance at her one last time before disappearing into the night, hoping she didn't catch sight of me. I'm getting careless, and it's a problem.

Chapter 5

Lena

I shake my head, trying to clear the dark thoughts from my mind. There's no way what I thought I saw was real. I swear a dark shadow was in the corner of the room, watching me pleasure myself, and I'm pretty sure it touched me. I felt something cool graze my wrist, making me tumble over the edge into my orgasm.

Most people would be terrified of what I imagined, but I found myself secretly hoping it was real. I felt drawn to the shadow in a way I can't explain. These dark urges inside me are a problem. I'm not only craving death but also picturing shadows in my apartment now.

I think about how the shadowy tendrils would hold me down and use my body for its every need. Fuck, thinking about being fucked by a shadow has me growing needy and wet again. What the hell is wrong with me?

I shake my head and look back over to the now empty corner. It was all in my head. I walk toward the bathroom to clean myself up and quickly pee before going back to bed. It's nearly 2am, and Carson still isn't home. You would think that after being a giant douche, making a sex tape about us, and letting some random girl release it to the entire campus, he would be doing a bit more groveling.

We still haven't spoken since I left yesterday. Maybe he is upset with me for not coming home. I deserve to have my time to deal with things. If I'm not ready to talk, then I shouldn't have to.

I glance down at my wrists and trail my finger over one of the now scabbed cuts. They weren't deep—just enough for the weight to free itself from my shoulders. I glance toward the bathroom. *I don't need to make it a habit again—it was just to get through the rough day.* I lay back down in bed, but my thoughts are on the blades in the bathroom. I crave the relief but hold out, allowing my drowsiness to pull me under.

A loud thump from across the room startles me awake. I shoot up in the bed, my heart pounding in my chest. "Carson?"

"Fuuuck, I diiidn'tt mean to wake yoou. Sorry," he slurs.

I glance down at my phone to see that it's nearly 4am. You have got to be kidding me.

"Where have you been all night?" I cross my arms over my chest.

"There wasss thiis party. Andd then theeere was this gi-iirl. Fuckkkk, I mean, you're theee girl I thoouught I saw. I do—don't know, Lenaaa. I'm drunkkkk. I need sleeeep."

He flops down on the bed next to me on his stomach after stripping to his boxers. Ice fills my veins as I replay his words in my head. There was a girl at the party. He was late because he was with someone else. Why else would he mention a girl? I glance over at him. It shouldn't matter. I'm not in love with Carson, but it hurts more than it should. I feel numb again, worthless.

It's another reminder that I don't mean anything to anyone. It's a lonely feeling, and the negative thoughts fill my mind. I should have never granted myself the freedom of the blade yesterday. Its call is so much stronger now that I've let myself succumb to it.

Carson is already snoring in the bed next to me. I could be anyone here with him right now, and he wouldn't give a shit. He doesn't need me. *Nobody needs me. The sooner I let myself just accept that again, the better off I'll be.*

I stand and stalk over to the bathroom, wondering if he will even bother questioning the marks on my arms when he wakes up hungover. My hands shake, and my heart slams in my chest, filling me with anticipation. I hid the blades in the cabinet under the sink after I came back from class earlier. I wanted them close in case I felt the pull that I'm feeling right now.

Reaching down, I open the cabinet and grab the pack, pulling out one of the shiny metal pieces. As I grip it in one hand, I glance at myself in the mirror. My eyes are wild, and my nostrils flare. My body aches for the release.

This is what makes me feel alive. I take a deep breath and glance down at my wrist before sliding the metal across it. I close my eyes and let the relief surge through me. When I open my eyes, I drag the blade across my skin again. I should have used the same arm as yesterday. That would have drawn less attention.

I only need two cuts tonight. It's still two more than I should have allowed myself. The blood drips from my wrist into the sink, and I stare at the crimson liquid. *If I were to end it all right now, would anyone care?* My mind swirls with the same thoughts that have plagued me for my entire life. *I don't mean anything to anyone. Nobody will ever need me, so why do I try so hard?* I blink through the dark thoughts.

I feel the sting from the peroxide I've poured over the cuts as I go through the motions blindly. Once the pain subsides, I rinse my wrist under the sink and tape the gauze I bought yesterday over it. It seems to be coming in handy more than I originally thought it would.

I take one last glance at my broken reflection in the mirror before going back to occupy the vacant space in bed next to Carson. I fall asleep quickly with the comfort of my self-inflicted wounds.

The morning sun peeks through the window, and the birds chirp cheerfully outside. I glance over to the space next to me in bed and find it empty. The clock shows it's nearly 10am, and I'm a bit shocked that I've slept that long.

My body must have been more exhausted from the emotions of the day than I originally thought. It's Saturday, so it doesn't matter much. I glance down at my wrist to see the bandage has lifted up on one side, allowing the air to scab over the cuts while I slept. There is a small blood stain on the bed, and I groan with the realization that I will have to throw the sheets out and buy new ones.

I step into the kitchen to find Carson fiddling with the coffee maker. "You're going to break it if you do that," I say as I walk toward him.

He turns to look at me, eyeing me in annoyance. "Feel free to do it then."

I scrunch up my face and furrow my brow at him. He is being more hostile than usual.

"You're pleasant today," I say as I slip past him to grab a mug and place it under the dispenser. I pull the frothier out of the way, add the necessary water, and push the start button. It's not that hard to work a fucking coffee maker.

"There's blood all over our sheets, Lena." His eyes land on my bandaged wrist, and then he looks back up at me. "What did you do to yourself? I don't understand how you can be fucked up enough to hurt yourself like that. When I started talking to you, you told me you stopped cutting. It's the only reason I even agreed with your parents to ask you out."

When I tell you I am shocked to my very core, that would be an understatement. My parents? What do my parents have to do with any of this? There's no way they would insert themselves in my life like that. Actually, that sounds about right, knowing them. I was leaving Cherry Hill, and they couldn't control me or my narrative anymore. This has my mother's name written all over it.

"What the fuck did you just say?" While I'm usually numb to emotions a good majority of the time, anger fills me over the prospect of my mother having any kind of say in my life anymore.

"Pretty sure you heard me loud and clear." He shrugs and pushes past me to grab the cup of coffee.

"I'm pretty sure I heard you say my parents were involved with us dating."

"Okay, good. You can at least hear properly." He pushes past me toward the living room, so I follow closely behind.

Everything over the last two days has just started stacking up. The video, the girl who sent it, the girl at the party, him coming home at 4am, him commenting on my cuts, my parents being the reason we're together—it's all too much.

"I'm not doing this with you anymore. We're done."

"Okay." He slumps down on the couch, reaching for the remote as if I didn't just break things off with him.

"I mean it, Carson. And I want to know if you have any more videos of the two of us that I have to worry about."

"I did you a favor by letting that get out. The other guys on campus might actually look your way now. Unfortunately, though, that was the only time I filmed us. With the shit you're into, I could probably make a killing selling them. If you're ever strapped for cash, let me know. I'll give you another good fucking."

I stand between him and the TV, crossing my arms over my chest. "I don't get it. Three days ago, you were all about making sure I was happy. You were the perfect little fake boyfriend for an entire year. Two days ago, you were practically begging me to forgive you for being the reason a sex tape was released. Now your tune has completely changed directions."

"Yeah, well, when I saw that fresh bullshit on your wrists, I realized you weren't worth the effort. You don't even like me. I'm pretty sure you know that I've been sleeping with other people for months now, and you haven't said anything about it. You just pretend to not notice."

"That's because I didn't notice, asshole." I shake my head in disgust. I knew I shouldn't have let myself cling to the idea of him for so long. I thought we could make it for the long haul, even though I wasn't in love with him. He was nice most of the time and has a decent career path. I figured if I was going to settle into life with someone, why not him?

"I'm over it now, Lena. You're not a girl a guy like me ends up with. You're fucked in the head, and nobody can fix you."

"Get out." I point toward the door.

He looks up at me and laughs. "Don't think so. This is my apartment until the end of the school year."

"You're just going to stay here then? I'm not leaving. I have nowhere else to go."

"Nobody said you had to leave. There are two bedrooms; just move your shit in there."

What in the actual fuck is going through this man's mind right now? I swear the Carson sitting in front of me today is a completely different person than the one I knew a few days ago. Maybe he was always like this, and I just didn't notice. We signed a lease when we moved in, both of us. I can't legally force him out.

"Why don't you go stay with whatever girl you were fucking last night?" I toss out. Part of me is baiting him to see if he will admit to being with another girl last night. I don't know why it matters. He has already proven he's a scumbag.

"Can't. She has a boyfriend."

"Well, isn't that just fucking perfect for her."

I glare at him one last time before storming out of the room to grab my purse, keys, and a few other things before I slam the apartment door behind me. I can't be in there with him right now. Fuck, how am I supposed to continue living with him?

Chapter 6

Kellan

It's been some time since she made any effort to pretend to like any of the people at Thorn Grove. After whatever Carson did to her, she spends most of her free time in the cemetery. It's been a week now of the same routine.

She goes to class, stops at her apartment while he is still in class to grab whatever she needs to occupy her time, and then drives here. She's always alone. She always has a sorrowful look on her face as she lays on her blanket in the grass or sits on the bench.

It's getting too cold for her to be out here doing this every day. It will snow soon. I watch her in my human form from behind one of the gravestones as she throws something in the air over and over again.

I get closer, trying not to draw attention to myself. She's on her back, with her black hair splayed across the blanket, tossing what appears to be a small purple and white ball. It has some kind of pattern, but I'm not close enough to see it.

She's singing something that I can't quite make out. I try to step closer to see if I can hear more of it, completely consumed by watching her every move. I mess up and step on a stick, causing a loud cracking noise to fill the air.

Her head snaps in my direction, and our eyes lock onto each other's. Those piercing brown eyes hold me in place as though she is a witch, and I am under her spell. My gaze never leaves hers as I walk forward. It's like an invisible force I can't control is pulling me closer to her.

"I didn't realize there was anyone else here," I lie.

"It's no bother." She pulls herself up to a seated position. I see curiosity written all over her face. I'm willing to bet she can feel the same electric pull that I feel between us. It's more intense than anything I've ever felt before.

I reach my hand down toward her, prompting her to shake it. "I'm Kellan. I'm sorry for bothering you. It seems like you were having a peaceful time."

Her eyes leave mine for the first time to look at my hand briefly before she glances back up at me. "Hi, Kellan. I'm Lena."

Her dainty hand reaches out to connect with mine, and time ceases to exist. My breath catches, and my eyes immediately dart to where the contact is being made. Sharp tingles course through me at her touch, lighting up my body and making me feel alive.

Death feeling alive. How about that?

Every part of me vibrates over the feel of her skin on mine. I glance back at her face to see that her lips have parted, and she is also staring at our connected hands. I knew she could feel it.

My perfect pet. She rips her hand out of my grasp and glances back up at me, eyes wide with shock.

"Have I seen you before?" her sweet voice coos.

"You may have seen me around campus."

"Oh." Her cheeks flush at the mention of the college. She's worried I've seen the video of her. I need to make sure she knows I'm not like the rest of them.

"I tend to keep to myself. I live off campus, and I don't have many interactions with people."

"You haven't seen the video of me getting railed by my ex-boyfriend then?" she blurts out. Her hand instantly covers her mouth as though she can't believe the words that just left her lips.

"I definitely haven't seen any video like that." It's not a lie. Although, I do have knowledge of the video she is speaking of. It brings my thoughts to the flushed look on her face after she fell apart on her fingers. I picture her with her legs spread open on the bed and her fingers rubbing relentlessly on her cunt. I have to focus to keep my cock from stirring in my pants.

She lets out a relieved laugh. "Want me to send it to you so you can join in on the laugh? Everyone else seems to be enjoying it."

I crouch down in front of her, and my gaze lands on her lips. "Seeing you with another man is of no interest to me." She gasps as I place two fingers under her chin, prompting her to lock eyes with me. "And I would never laugh at you. With you, yes, but never at you."

Her eyes flick down to my lips, and I have to resist the urge to lean forward and press them to hers. For a moment, we are one wavelength traveling through time together. Each of us is entirely consumed by the presence of the other. It's like nothing I've ever experienced in my entire existence.

Before she can lean in further, I stand up and gesture to her blanket. "Do you mind if I sit with you? I don't know many people who enjoy spending time in the graveyard. I would love to know more about you."

A soft smile spreads across her lips. "I think I would like that." Her cheeks flush the slightest shade of pink, and I find myself wanting to make her feel like this more often. The color looks so contradictory on her porcelain skin. She moves over and allows me to take residence next to her.

It's odd being so close to her. The desire to make her mine is stronger than ever. I can sense the way she dissects and analyzes my every move. She is just as curious about me as I am about her.

We spend the next few hours talking to one another, and I am transfixed by everything she tells me. Even after watching her from a distance for so long, there is so much I don't know.

Her favorite food is pizza, and her favorite candy is Werther's Originals. She loves the color purple, especially purple tulips, but she has only received flowers a few times in her life. I'll have to rectify that.

While I love knowing these things about her, I want her to know that I wish to know the true her, not just surface-level

                    K.M. BAKER

things about her. It's getting close to sunset, and our time to-gether is running out. I take a calculated risk and point to the scars on her wrist.

"When did you start?" I ask, not leaving it up for interpretation as to what I'm talking about. Her eyes glint with vulnerability, and she squeezes the ball she was tossing earlier. At a closer glance, it has a galaxy pattern to it.

"I was twelve the first time." She averts her gaze as if she is ashamed to admit this to me.

I reach out and grip her chin, pulling her eyes back to me. "You don't have to be ashamed of who you are, Lena."

Softness flashes across her face, but as quickly as it appears, it disappears. "You don't know anything about who I am."

"Tell me, then. I want to know everything about you. I can't explain it, but I have a need to know you." I inch my face forward. All I want right now is to press my lips against hers in an attempt to dissipate every ounce of stubbornness from her soul. She's not normally like this. "I know you feel the same pull I do. You wouldn't have let me sit here with you for the last several hours if you didn't. There's something here connecting us. I don't understand it any more than you do."

My hand slides along her face, and I rest it at the base of her neck near her collarbone. I lean in further and lightly brush my lips against hers, feeling the way her pulse quickens under my fingertips. Her eyes lock on mine, and she leans in the rest of the way to press her lips against mine.

If I could die, I think I would right now. Tasting her is far beyond anything I could have ever imagined. Life fills every fiber of my being, lighting me up and causing a high I've never felt before. I need more of her.

My hand slips around the back of her neck, and I pull her closer to deepen the kiss. Her tongue dances with mine as we lose ourselves in one another. She nips at my bottom lip, and I bring my other hand up to rest it on her cheek, savoring her.

She moves toward me, throwing one leg over my lap and straddling me. I almost lose the ability to breathe. Having her on me like this is enough for me to forget who I am entirely. I've forgotten that I'm not supposed to be involving myself in human lives, but talking to her changed everything. She is my only purpose. I was made for her, and she was made for me.

I tangle my fingers in her black hair and pull her lips off mine so I can lean in and kiss up the length of her neck. She groans in response, grinding her pussy on my erect cock. I long to be inside her. I pepper her neck with kisses, relishing in how her skin seems to taste like everything I never knew I was missing out on.

"Is this what you want?" she whispers in my ear, and that question forces me to withdraw from her.

Yes, I want her more than anything, but not like this. I want every piece of her and having her like this right now would only make her think I was after her body, not her mind and soul. She stares at me with curiosity, and I run my knuckles along her cheek reassuringly.

"Would you tell me about them?" I lightly tap on her wrist, avoiding the new cuts.

Her eyes bounce back and forth between mine as if she's trying to make sure I am really asking about her and not just trying to find a way to trick her. Ultimately, she nods. She goes to slip off of my lap, but I grip her hips, holding her in place. I'm not ready to stop feeling her body pressed against mine.

She gulps and brings her left arm up to the side of us. We both glance over at it. "I was twelve, and my grandma just died. She was my entire world. My parents weren't exactly the most loving people to grow up with. My mother was always more concerned with outward appearances, and my father just never cared. I spent a lot of time with my grandma. She was warm, loving, and the only place I was ever able to find true happiness."

She trails off, lowering her gaze as though it pains her to talk about it. I wait for her to find the strength she needs to continue, not moving a single portion of my body. I am invested in finding out about this part of her. I'm not going to run when things feel tense or uncomfortable. She will learn that. Finally, she looks back over at her wrist again.

"It was after my grandma's funeral. I tried to talk to my mom, but she didn't care. Her own mother died, and she acted like nothing happened. It was the first time I felt truly alone. I spent all my time with my grandma and only had one other friend, Dani, whom I wasn't extremely close to at the time. My mom forced me to go to my grandma's house and sort through some of her things after I told her I didn't want to be there. It was too hard. I was in her bathroom, and I happened to look over to see a razor blade sitting on the sink. I stared at them for a while, wondering what it would feel like to die so that I could be with her."

She chokes on her words, tears threatening to fall from her eyes. "It's okay. I'm here," I say reassuringly.

"I had nobody. My mom always made me feel like a burden. It was the first time I thought I might be better off dead than alive. I grabbed the razor blade and thought maybe if I hurt myself, I could feel something other than the pain of her death, so I did. I slid it against my wrist so lightly that it barely broke the surface and then dropped the blade in the sink. I stared at the cut for a while and realized I liked the release it gave me."

I can tell that was hard for her to admit. It's almost as though this is the first time she is talking out loud about how she feels about it. "There's nothing wrong with the way you felt, Lena."

"I've been doing it off and on since then. It makes me feel like I'm in control. I'm the only one who can inflict pain when I cut myself. I get to choose how badly it hurts. I get to choose how long it will hurt. I get the control over when I want to end it all." She looks up at me, broken and exposed. "It makes me feel something in a world where I've spent so much time feeling nothing at all."

I ache to comfort her, to hold her, and tell her everything is going to be okay no matter what. I want to tell her she never has to be alone ever again. I hold back because she just met me tonight, and I don't want to risk scaring her away.

"Thank you for sharing that with me. I know it must not have been easy. If it's worth anything at all, I think you're incredibly strong. It takes a lot for a person to be able to admit something like you just did."

She leans into me, resting her head on my shoulder. I wrap my arms around her back and hold her in a close hug. This moment right here is everything. Having her in my arms to hold and comfort is better than I ever imagined.

"Kellan, what is this pull between us? I don't understand why I feel so comfortable around you after we just met. I've never felt like this."

"Sometimes two beings are just meant to find comfort in one another," I admit.

She sighs, like she wants to further question my statement, but she doesn't. She simply relaxes further into my hold, and the two of us watch as the sun sets and the darkness engulfs us.

Chapter 7

Lena

Meeting Kellan in the graveyard was unexpected. Something about him seems so familiar, but I can't place it. Up until today, he was a stranger that I've never seen, yet for some reason, I feel safe around him. Maybe I shouldn't have let things progress as far as I did tonight. Something about him called out to the very core of my soul.

I was lying there on the blanket, tossing my stress ball, thinking about how easy it would be to die. My mom would make some big show over how hard everything is for her and how she just doesn't understand where she went wrong with raising me. My father would whine about the cost of everything. Since Dani and I cut things off, I don't have any real friends. Lexi is there sometimes, but she's always been a friend of convenience. We talk about boys and school, that's about it. It's all surface-level.

As soon as my gaze locked with Kellan's green eyes, every thought I had of worthlessness and despair disappeared. Time seemed to freeze around me. In his presence, death was no longer something I yearned for. My mind was quiet, and the urges dissipated.

He brought me a peace I've always longed for. It's uncanny, really. This one person has the ability to make me feel the way I've always wanted throughout my life. Is this what being normal feels like? We talked for hours about so many things, and he just listened. Nobody has been willing to listen for such a long time.

I hold my arm out, looking down at the unhealed cuts along my wrists, and remember the way his skin felt against mine. It was like a surge of electricity pumping through my veins. I've never felt so free and alive.

Then, there was the gentle way in which he asked about the scars. He genuinely wanted to know. He wasn't looking to make fun of me or judge me. He told me he would never laugh at me. Something in me believes in that more than anything I've ever believed in before. I stayed at the cemetery with him until the sun set, and we reluctantly parted ways.

As soon as he left my line of sight, all of the feelings of worthlessness and despair came rushing back in, crashing upon me. It was almost some sort of validation that he was the one keeping the feelings at bay. I found myself standing there for a while after he left, wishing he would come back and take it all away again.

Reluctantly, I loaded myself into my car and came back to my apartment. When I walked inside, I found out Carson had already left for the evening, thankfully. Since breaking things off, we have been doing a pretty successful job of avoiding one another. I have no desire to see him and have nothing but pure distaste for him.

I don't understand why he insists on living here. It's been a week since we broke up, and he's made no effort to leave. He has plenty of friends and teammates on campus that he could move in with until the end of the school year. I'm convinced his main goal in life is to torture me as much as possible. Fucker.

With a sigh, I crash into my new bed. I moved all of my things to the second bedroom as soon as I could. I had absolutely no desire to stay in the room we shared.

I lay in bed and stare up at the ceiling, wondering how the fuck I'm supposed to get through the rest of this school year with him living here. If I had any kind of self-respect, I would suck it up and ask my parents for help. My dad makes more than enough money- to afford putting me up in a new apartment.

It's just more complicated than simply asking for something with them. Asking my parents means having a conversation about Carson and me breaking up. The guy that my mother freaking set me up with. She probably paid him to date me so she didn't have to live with the shame of her weird daughter still being single.

I won't talk to them. My mother will get her text every few days, and that's it. The fact that she found a way to involve herself in my romantic life pisses me off. Anger is a better emotion than despair and the longing to die. I've been feeling a lot of anger lately. I suppose I'm making progress, right? My mother would be so proud.

I let myself drift off to sleep with thoughts of my parents, their meddling, and how I'm supposed to move forward with the rest of this school year. All problems that I will, no doubt, push off and avoid.

Darkness surrounds me, and I feel as though I'm drowning. There is no peace here. There is no happiness. It's as if everything I've been feeling while awake has manifested itself into my worst nightmare.

Screams tear through my mind as I walk down a dark hallway. There is a pale light toward the very end that I covet. It seems peaceful there. I want to get out of this darkness more than I've ever wanted anything, but it's no use. No matter how far or fast I walk, the light never gets closer. It always stays just out of reach.

The walls start to close in around me, and panic swells in my chest. I crave safety so I run faster, trying to escape the inevitable fate of the walls squeezing in around me.

Just as I feel like there is no hope, a figure appears in my path. I can't see who they are through the darkness, but there is no turning back. I have to keep moving forward. I run toward them and catch a glint of their bright, shining eyes staring back at me.

The aura around the figure is dark but it calls to me. As I move ahead, I notice the light is finally getting closer. It's almost like the dark figure is bringing me to the light. As the figure comes into focus, it's not really in focus at all. It is a moving cloud of smoke with tendrils splaying out from it.

One of the tendrils inches toward me. I should be afraid, but it seems so inviting. I finally step forward into the light as a hand emerges from the shadow and grips my throat. Instead of reaching out to try to get it off of me, I run my fingers along the shadowy hand in a caressing manner.

I'm pushed up against a white wall that seems to have appeared out of nowhere, and the figure takes shape in front of me. The cloudy smoke dissipates in some places, and an outline of a man in a cloak takes its place. The man has no concrete features outside of the deep green eyes that stare into mine. Eyes that look so familiar. It's all white around us now.

I look up as my chest rises and falls with rapid breaths. Fingers tighten around my throat, and I feel something sliding up the length of my leg. I try to glance down, but I'm unable to move my head with the hand gripping it.

"I bet you're already so wet and needy," a voice emits from the figure. It's sultry and sexy. Hypnotizing in its own sort of way. The voice is right. I'm already turned on. I long for it to use me and call me a dirty slut in the process.

"Please," I whine as the grip on my neck loosens.

I look down to see the shadow sliding closer to my center. I'm completely naked somehow. Why am I so turned on by this? I should be freaking out, but I'm not fighting back at all. Just as I find myself starting to wonder what the hell I'm thinking, a light pressure slides across my center.

My head falls back against the wall, and all of the cells in my body come to life. A soft moan slips from my lips, and I find myself tilting my hips forward, silently craving more. The half-human, half-smoke figure steps into me, and I feel my feet being kicked apart.

"*What are you?*" I whisper as I look up, trying to make out some of the features of its face. The smoke makes it difficult to make out anything tangible.

"*Do you want to talk, or do you want me to fuck you?*" the figure says.

Without answering, I bring my hand up and place it on a firm chest. The smoke around it dissolves enough to reveal strong muscles before me. I slide my hand down further to wrap it around a hard cock, just briefly, before something wraps around my wrist and pulls my hand free from his shaft.

Both of my wrists are pulled above my head, and I'm lifted off the ground, away from the wall. I try to kick my feet, but my ankles are pulled apart. I glance down to see shadowy tendrils holding my suspended form in place. I am completely at his whim, and the anticipation races through me. My heart beats rapidly as I wait for the shadow man's next move.

"*Be a good girl for me, and let me fuck you.*"

A finger swipes along my wet pussy, and any objective thoughts free my mind. I moan loudly as his finger slips inside me. He begins pumping it in and out slowly. I thrust my hips forward, aiding him in the process, needing more.

"*I knew you would be a soaking wet slut for me.*" He growls.

"More," I whine.

"*Look at you, so needy for the darkness. Are you not afraid of me?*" he asks as he adds a second finger.

I should be afraid, but I'm not. I fucking crave every single second of it, wishing he would push my limits further.

"I'm not afraid," I breathe out.

A chuckle rumbles from his chest. "You should be."

His fingers move faster, rubbing my walls and building up the desire within. I gasp when I feel something else pushing its way inside my pussy alongside his fingers. It's almost like he read my mind.

"Are you afraid now, pet?"

I look down to see one of his shadowy tendrils between my legs. He finger fucks me faster in tandem with the shadow. His thumb finds my clit, and everything inside me starts to build. I feel so much pleasure coming from so many places.

His shadow face leans in to bite down on my neck. I would run my fingers along his back if I could move my wrists. If this was real, instead of a dream, I would have marks up the length of my neck tomorrow.

"Give it to me, pet. Give me all of your pleasure, like the dirty slut you love being."

His words fuel something inside me, and the desire begins to spread. His fingers move faster, and the shadow curves inside me, hitting the perfect spot. I see stars.

My body erupts, sending heat coursing to my core. My eyes roll back as electricity shoots down my arms and legs to my fingers and toes. My pussy spasms, and I clamp down on both his shadow and fingers, letting my orgasm consume me. He groans and continues his pace until my body finally begins to come down.

I look into his eyes, and I swear I've seen them before. I don't have a chance to question it further, though, because my attention is drawn to something else.

He pulls everything out of me, leaving me empty for a brief moment, and spins me around. My wrists are pulled forward, and I'm bent in half, still being held up in the air. Another tendril now wraps around my waist for further support. Before I have a moment to complain, his hard cock is sliding into me inch by inch. He's so much bigger than anyone I've ever been with, and I love the way my pussy stretches around him.

"Fuck," I cry out as he seats himself fully inside me.

"Your pussy is so fucking tight, pet."

A hand slams down on one of my ass cheeks, and I scream. It's so dirty, but I love every second of it. He slaps the other cheek before leaning down to whisper in my ear. "Mine."

He starts moving inside me, and I've never felt anything more heavenly. One of his hands reaches around to roll my nipple between his fingers as he slams into me from behind.

"Yes!" I moan.

His free hand slaps down on my ass again, giving me the perfect mixture of pain and pleasure. It has my pussy pulsing for him. It's almost as though he knows exactly how I want him to use my body.

He spits on my ass, and I feel a tendril swirl the wetness around my back hole. Before I have a chance to object, it slips into me slowly. The shadow slowly makes itself larger, stretching me out while he continues to pump in and out of both of my holes.

His hand slaps my ass again. "That's it. Take it all like a desperate slut."

"Please," I whimper. I don't even know what I'm asking for at this point.

"You like being fucked in all your holes, don't you?" he asks, as the shadow moves in and out of my ass in sync with his cock.

"I love it!" I admit.

"Such a good fucking girl for me. As soon as this pussy coats my cock with your come, it'll always belong to me. Would you like that, Lena? Do you want to belong to me?"

"I don't even know who you are," I admit.

"That's not what I asked." He slams into me harder. His fingers pinch my nipple again, and I feel another orgasm creeping up on me. There are just so many things happening all at once. It's hard to keep my body in check.

"It's too much," I pant.

"Come on my cock, pet. Let me watch you become mine."

I can't even protest because my body barrels toward the edge at a pace I'm not able to keep up with. My heart slams as the pleasure threatens to work its way through me. He slides in and out of me, one, two, three, more times before I lose it all.

Tingles overtake my body as I find my blissful high. It feels so much fucking better than anything I've ever felt before. I clamp down hard around his cock as my entire world shatters and satisfaction fills me.

"That's a good fucking girl," he says before I feel something shooting inside me. He groans as he leans into his pleasure, and we both ride out the high together.

"You're perfect for me" is the last thing I hear before I wake up panting as I frantically look around the room to find myself alone. A shred of disappointment fills me when I realize the whole delicious string of events was nothing more than a figment of my apparently very active dreams.

It all felt so real. The soaking wet mess between my legs makes me feel like it was real. I must have actually come in my sleep. The worst part about it is that I fucking loved every minute of it.

I shake my head and throw off the covers to clean myself up in the bathroom. I need to get these thoughts under control. I don't know what's going on with me lately. Hallucinating the shadow figure in the corner, and now fucking it in my dreams.

Chapter 8

Kellan

After I walked away from her in the cemetery, I knew the few hours I spent with her weren't enough. I shouldn't have involved myself in the way I did. I should have apologized for disturbing her and walked away, but she was just too hard to resist. And after I tasted her, I needed more.

She went back to her apartment and fell asleep. When I popped in to check on her, she was clearly in the midst of a nightmare. I had to invade her dreams to ensure she was okay. I don't want my pet suffering, even in her unconscious state, if I can help it. I'm not sure if it goes against the rules, but I've found myself wanting to break the rules more and more with her. Technically, dreams are not reality, so they don't count—a pleasant loophole.

I'm so glad I did, too. The way she came apart on my cock was unlike anything I've ever experienced. I only wish that it could have been in real life and not in a dream. Something about her thinking of our first time as a dream doesn't sit well with me.

I want her to know she belongs to me. My sweet pet who comes so beautifully. I want to make her pussy squeeze my cock as I fill all of her holes as often as possible. She loves being degraded, and I'm happy to oblige. I shake my head, remembering the sequence of events and vowing to find a way to feel her in that way again. It's a new day, and I'm sure she will wake up more than satisfied.

I've been neglecting my duties, and I've had so much to catch up on this morning. For the first time, I wonder what would happen if I didn't show up to guide the souls to my realm. Would someone show up in my absence? Would they find their own way somehow?

All souls have a path they ultimately have to take. I wonder just how important my role in all of this truly is. I was expecting some sort of recourse for delaying the souls I was supposed to guide last night, but there was none. Due to my distraction, they were simply granted a few extra hours in the mortal world.

Lena is all I'm able to think about anymore. Even while working this morning, the only thing running through my mind was the way she placed her hand on my chest in her dream. I long for that touch in real life. Her hand is warm and soft, and I crave it.

She's changing me, and there's no going back to the being I was before her. I want to shield her from hurt and the pain. I want to be the shoulder she leans on, the place she runs to when things get tough. I want her to finally feel like she has something to look forward to for the first time in so long.

She doesn't need the blade to make her feel. I can do that for her. I just need to find a way to help her see it. I'll deal with the consequences of everything else along the way. I won't ever willingly let her feel alone again.

I take on my human form, dressed in a pair of blue jeans, a black long-sleeve shirt, and a pair of Converse, before heading toward campus. I want to stage this perfectly so we run into each other. She's not ready to know exactly how long I've been obsessing over her yet. Someday, I will confess everything to her, but not today.

I know the exact path she walks from her second to third class when she gets lunch. Today, I'm going to intercept her. Hopefully, she will agree to let me join her. The other students are still making comments about her here and there under their breath, and she pretends it doesn't bother her, but I can see the pain behind her eyes.

I shouldn't seek her out again. This is a dangerous game I'm playing. If I involve myself too much, it could interfere with her purpose, but I do it anyway. I walk from the corner of the building, placing myself directly in her path. She's just a few steps in front of me, getting ready to walk past.

"Kellan?" she calls out almost immediately.

I lock eyes with her and stop in my tracks, waiting for her to close the distance between us. Hearing my true name on her lips is the most glorious sound I think I've ever heard. I long to hear her say it over and over again.

"Lena?" I question. I have to make this appear to be an accident.

"What are the chances I run into you again so soon?"

"It's a smaller campus than you think," I say, not wanting to admit I've been waiting here for her and that this run-in wasn't exactly by chance. "How are you doing today?"

She glances around at all the people looking our way. They are curious. She's been keeping to herself since the video was released. Her breakup with Carson didn't go unnoticed. If anything, it brought even more attention to her during a time when she was trying to stay invisible.

I reach out to touch her arm reassuringly. "I don't care what they think."

Her eyes meet mine again, and time stops. It's just the two of us lost to the universe within one another. Her shoulders visibly relax, and she seems to breathe easier as a faint smile spreads across her face.

"Are you sure? They have a lot of opinions about me."

"The only opinion I care about is yours. I don't give a fuck about any of them," I reassure her, and it's the truth.

Fuck. Did I just say fuck? I've never felt the need to curse outside of my thoughts before, but it felt nice slipping off my tongue. She is transforming me into an entirely new being full of complex emotions and feelings. The Others will not be happy about this. The Others can fuck right off.

"Would you like to join me for lunch, or are you heading to class? You might not care what everyone thinks, but I've had enough stares this week to last a lifetime." She rubs the sides of her covered arms anxiously.

"Let's go grab something to eat. I have some time before I have anywhere to be."

I reach out my hand in front of her, prompting her to take it, and her breath hitches at the sight. She hesitates for a brief moment, looking up at me with eyes full of vulnerability as her chest rises and falls rapidly.

Nervousness fills me. What if she doesn't accept my gesture? Maybe she thought what she told me in the cemetery would scare me off or that I wasn't being sincere. I'm not sure how I would cope with her rejecting me. I give her a slight nod of reassurance, hoping that it will encourage her to trust me.

She intertwines her fingers with mine, and the moment we touch, everything around us changes. The grass looks greener. The sun shines brighter. The fresh smell of the air is more potent than ever. Chills run through me at the contact. I never want to let her go.

"I'm glad I ran into you," she confesses as I lead her to the dining hall.

Nobody else around us matters anymore. The only person she can see is me, and vice versa. Nothing can change the way the two of us feel. We still barely know each other, but we are made for one another.

"I'm glad, too," I admit.

Once we enter the dining hall, we grab our food and find a small booth in the corner of the room where we will have the least amount of prying eyes. I'm sure people are wondering who I am and if she is already slutting herself out to a new man.

Humans can't help but be curious, but it's none of their damn business. I would love to give them all finality in order to protect my pet from another demeaning word leaving their mouths. I can't do that, though. The Others would notice. I'm surprised they haven't shown themselves to me already.

I am almost positive spending the afternoon with Lena yesterday changed her path in one way or another. Kissing her definitely changed things. I'm grateful they haven't tried to interfere. Maybe they are waiting to see if I will do the right thing. The only right thing is for me to be with Lena.

The Others are the only beings who can change the outcome of the souls I am destined to collect and those in my realm. While I call them The Others, most people know them as God and the Devil. They are the only beings with the potential to override death.

I've never done anything that would draw their attention before because I've always been a neutral bystander. As of yesterday, in the graveyard with Lena, I have officially diverted from neutrality.

Soon enough, each of them will send their spokesperson to me in an attempt to get me back on the path I'm meant for. The problem with that is that Lena is now the only path I'm interested in. I'm sure some kind of punishment will ensue from it. My only hope is that I have enough time to figure out what to do before they send their lackeys my way.

She takes another bite of her sandwich, staring at me as I push around the pasta on my plate. We've been sitting here in silence, willing the other to start up the conversation first. Both of us long to be in one another's presence but also share the same difficulty of how to act in a social setting.

"You're staring." I grin.

"Maybe a little. You're nice to stare at, though."

"I'm glad I'm easy on the eyes." I grab my drink and take a sip. "What are you going to school for?"

"Business. I wasn't sure what I wanted to do when I got out of college. I figured a business degree would be the easiest option."

"You don't seem like the business type, no offense."

"I think my father would agree with that." She laughs.

"Your father?" This is the first time she's spoken about him to me. I'm curious what she will say. I know he has extremely high and unrealistic expectations for her.

"Yeah, he's all about business and money. He made sure to let me know that he had no plans to let me run his business. I mean, I'm still not entirely sure what he does, but it doesn't change the fact that I'll never be good enough for him."

"What do you mean?"

"He's always intended to marry me off so that he can pass his company along to his son-in-law. The only thing I've ever been good for, in his eyes, was ensuring the next generation of fucked up men."

"Your father sounds like an asshole."

"Yeah, he is. Anyway, him being so shitty fueled me. I want a business degree even more. I want to prove him wrong. I have no clue if I'll even use the degree, but even if I don't, it will be a nice little fuck you to my father."

"I like the way you think." I smile as she brings a bottle of water to her mouth. My breath catches when her tongue dips out to lick the few drops that wet her lips. "Your father is out of his mind if he doesn't realize your worth."

"Thank you for that. You're the first person to make me feel something good in a really long time. You seem to be the first person to see me for who I am, and you still barely know me."

Reassuringly, I reach my hand out and place it on top of hers.

"Does that sound completely insane? I swear I'm not ever like this with everyone. There's something about you that I feel drawn to," she confesses.

"That doesn't sound insane at all. I feel the same way. I've never felt an intense desire to be near someone until I laid eyes on you."

"It doesn't make any sense." She shakes her head in an attempt to rationalize the pull we feel toward one another.

"Not everything is supposed to make sense. Let's take it day by day and see how things go."

"Okay."

It's right there on the tip of my tongue. I'm so close to asking her to be mine, but I don't think she is ready for that yet. She is still confused, and I want her to find comfort in me, not fear me. I'll give her the space, for right now at least, to explore what these feelings mean. I know her mental health isn't the best, and I never want to pressure her.

She glances down at her phone and then back at me with wide eyes. "I'm so sorry to leave you this quickly, but I only have a few minutes before my next class. I didn't realize how long we've been here."

I smile at her. "It's okay. Get to class. We can finish talking another time."

"How will I get a hold of you? " She stands and gathers her things to throw away in the nearby trash can.

"I'm sure we will run into each other, but we can plan to meet at this time every day if that helps. You never have to eat lunch alone again."

"That sounds perfect."

She goes to step away from the table, but I reach out to grab her arm one last time before she goes. "I'll see you tomorrow, Lena."

"See you tomorrow, Kellan," she says, and I lean down to kiss her on the cheek, watching the pink hue fill them.

As she leaves to go to her last class of the day, I feel an emptiness overtaking me. It's as though she is solely responsible for every piece of life blooming inside me. Without her, I am simply nothing, nobody, death. This one woman makes me feel like I am somebody.

She gives life to death. My entire being begins and ends with her.

I find myself wondering what I'm going to do when my time with her ultimately runs out. We are on a clock, and time is not on our side. I can't keep her. I remind myself, but I sure as fuck will find a way to change this. My perfect pet. She feels the same way toward me. I just know it. I'll find an exception so she can stay with me forever. With that final thought, I disappear to perform the day's duties I have been neglecting.

Chapter 9

Lena

I find myself thinking of Kellan as I pull up to the cemetery. We've been getting lunch every day for the last three weeks now, and he's become the part of my daily routine that I desire the most. My classes are over for the day, and I need some time to decompress before returning to my apartment.

There is a bitter chill in the air, and although it hasn't snowed yet, early winter seems to be upon us. Where will I go once there's snow on the ground, and it's too cold to lay out here on my blanket? I guess I can sit in my car, but that's not exactly peaceful.

I glance around at the headstones before throwing my blanket on the ground and grabbing my purple stress ball. Things have been going well, almost too well, for three weeks now. I wonder when the other shoe is going to drop. My life is never easy like this. When good things happen, it's usually a preface for something awful.

Kellan coming into my life was a welcomed surprise. He understands me in a way I can't describe. He takes the time to ask about me and listens. I've never met anyone who listens as well as he does. For most of my life, I've craved death. Even now, a part of me craves it, but it's been silenced by the peace he brings. When I'm in his presence, everything goes away.

He's been incredibly respectful, and I like that. Things between us haven't progressed any further than a chaste kiss here and there. It reassures me that he's not trying to get in my pants. At this point, I might let him. Earlier this week, I opened my car to find the most gorgeous purple tulips I've ever seen in my life. When I asked him about them, he said I deserved something almost as beautiful as I am. He got them because he knows they are my favorite.

People don't think about me the same way he does. They don't take the time to make sure I'm happy. It feels nice but wrong all at the same time. How can I so willingly let him treat me so well when my mind is still so fucked up? I ruin everything. I try not to, but the bad thoughts always find a way to push themselves to the forefront of my mind.

Even now, thinking about him and how sweet he's been, I still find myself focusing on the possibility of something terrible happening. Is there something going on that I don't know about? It's all too good to be true. Will I be on the bathroom floor again with slices down my wrists?

I shake my head to clear the negative thoughts. He has been the biggest blessing I've had in a long time. Outside of our lunch dates, we've been meeting up here in the cemetery a few nights a week. He just shows up, and I don't mind one bit. Every moment with him feels like it will never be enough. I've grown attached to him in a way I don't like to admit.

I take a deep breath and focus on the way he makes me feel, tossing the stress ball into the air for the next few hours. I watch as the clouds float above, and I know it's almost time for me to go back to my apartment. I'm dreading it. With a sigh, I sit up and gather my things before returning to my car. I sure as fuck hope Carson is out and about fucking whoever lets him between her legs and not at the apartment.

I've been pretty successful in avoiding him for a month now. I come home and go to sleep before he makes his grand entrance sometime after midnight. When I wake up, he is still passed out from his escapades, so I leave. It's become a perfect routine, but I know it's only a matter of time before it ends. I've been too lucky, and I don't get lucky.

After a quick drive to my apartment, I park the car and take one last deep breath before making my way inside. As I slide the key in, I hear a noise on the other side of the door and roll my eyes. Apparently, my luck has just run out. I'm about to have my first face-to-face run-in with the asshole.

I push open the door and try to walk to my bedroom as fast as possible. If I can get in there and avoid any kind of conversation, that would be ideal. I freeze when I hear a giggle in the hallway.

"She was weird as fuck anyway and never really appreciated you," the familiar female voice says.

"Do you appreciate me?" Carson asks her.

"You know I do, baby."

"You've definitely had a good way of showing it over the last two weeks."

"I want to feel you, Carson," she whines.

"Fuck, you're so damn tight," Carson tells her.

I march toward the sound, not giving a fuck what I'm about to see. Who do they think they are? What makes her think she is so much better than me? I see nothing but red as I turn the corner, and they come into view.

"Lexi, what the fuck?" I shout, standing there with my lip curled up in disgust and my arms crossed over my chest.

"I didn't think you were into voyeurism, Lena. I'm a little busy here. Unless your eyes are broken, you can probably see I'm balls-deep in Lexi at the moment." Carson turns his head in my direction, locking eyes with me as he continues to drive his cock in and out of my supposed best friend's pussy. He has her pinned against the wall with her dress pushed up and her panties pulled to the side.

"Fuck you. This is my apartment."

"Watch if you want then. Maybe it'll give you something to cut yourself to after I leave."

My eyes almost pop out of my head over how blunt he is. How can he be so crass about something like that?

"You really are a piece of shit with no regard for anyone except yourself."

"The blades are on the sink waiting for you," he calls out as I turn on my heels to get the fuck out of here. Tears threaten to soak my cheeks, but I don't want to give him the satisfaction of seeing them.

"Lena?" Lexi tries, and I pause, turning to look at her for just a moment. Guilt crosses her face before Carson plunges back inside her, and the guilty look transforms back to lust. I give her a quick middle finger and run out of the apartment and back to my car.

My mind is only focused on one thing. I take the familiar drive to the store and grab the same things I did just a few weeks prior. I feel so overwhelmed with everything as I drive back to the cemetery. My refuge. When I arrive, I mindlessly grab my blanket and the contents from the store and walk back to my favorite bench.

Lexi was just letting my ex fuck her in MY apartment. I know we weren't the closest people in the world, but her willingness to do that just proves she doesn't care about me at all. I open the blanket and lay on it, trying to think about Kellan. Maybe that will change this worthless feeling to something more positive. If he were here, he would comfort me. *He's not here, though. You're alone like always.* I blink, staring out into the distance. Some people just aren't meant for happiness. I'm not meant to be happy. The dark thoughts in my mind are too strong. I can't fight them.

The self-doubt takes over, and I lose control. The sun begins to set. I should focus on the beauty of the sky rather than the empty feeling in my soul. I reach into the new package of blades and quickly grab one before pushing up the sleeves of my sweater. A quick glance at my wrist shows the faint lines of every cut I've inflicted upon myself. Memories of each one flood my thoughts.

I look them over, contemplating where to place the new ones. The thicker scars draw my attention, reminding me of that day on my bathroom floor two years ago. Why couldn't I just finish the job then? I settle on a spot a few inches below my wrist and push the blade to my skin. It's the exact reaction Carson wanted, but I can't stop myself. My brows raise, and tears fall from my face as the blade bites into my flesh and gives me the relief I seek. It's my attempt to take control of my feelings.

I wish Kellan were here. My chest heaves as I close my eyes to try and level out my thoughts. *Shut them off. Just don't feel.* It's all too much. I'm so lost and alone. I'm tired of always feeling like this. I trail the sharp metal along my wrist again as the tears fall freely, soaking my face.

I sit here like this for a while. I should bandage the cuts, but I don't have it in me right now. I slump my head down in defeat, watching as the blood drips down my arms and onto the blanket. I don't know what else to do except cry, alone and broken.

"Lena?" Kellan's voice calls out, and my empty eyes lift to meet his.

He doesn't say anything else. He simply sits down next to me, reaches over, and pulls me into him. His arms wrap around my center, and I go still for a moment before allowing myself to relax into his hold. A strangled sob leaves me, and he holds me tighter. As soon as I'm in his arms, the feelings of doubt, pain, and worthlessness seem to disappear, like they always do.

"It's okay. I've got you," he says reassuringly as one of his hands rubs small circles on my back.

I finally give in and wrap my arms around his waist, letting him comfort me. He doesn't ask me what happened. He doesn't mention the cuts on my wrist, the blood-soaked blanket, or the blades in the open package sitting next to me. He doesn't judge me like everyone else does. He just comforts me, and I relish the calming feeling he provides.

Chapter 10
Kellan

Every stolen moment with her is not enough. I've grown annoyed with how often I'm called away from her to perform my duties. For the first time in my existence, I wish I wasn't who I am. I wish I could be just a normal soul who gets to spend a lifetime with her and have the memories to go along with it. Instead, I am haunted by the knowledge that our time is growing closer to ending with every breath she takes.

If The Others try to take her from me, I'll stop them. What would they do if she wanted to stay with me? How would they react to that? What if her purpose all along was to be mine for eternity?

A sickening feeling washes over me as I lead the last soul from my list to my realm. Something isn't right with Lena, and I need to hurry this along and get back to her. A dark, anxious feeling creeps over me just as I usher the soul forward so they can carry on with their purpose. As soon as they set off on their own, I fade away from their sight and seek out my girl.

She is in the cemetery, but it's late. She shouldn't be here this late. Normally by now, she has gone back to her apartment. I take on my human form and move along the tombstones in the dusk toward her usual spot. She comes into view, and my eyes widen. She is trembling with her head down, staring at her bloody wrist. When her eyes finally lift up to meet mine, it breaks something in me.

I don't ever want her to be helpless like this again. I've failed to protect her. I want to fucking eviscerate whoever made her feel like this. Immediately, I pull her close and reassure her that I'm here. She sinks into my hold and lets herself fall apart in the safety of my arms.

After some time, she lifts up her head and looks at me. "How did you know I was here?"

"You like coming here. I was in the area, so I thought I would see if you were still here. I'm glad I did."

"Yeah, I'm glad you did too." She moves to a seated position

I should confess everything to her. Lay it all on the line to see if she is willing to choose me over everything. The Others would have to consider things differently if she knew the truth, but I can't bring myself to do it yet.

"Why did I never notice you before? You're always around now," she whispers.

"Sometimes, once you see something, it's hard not to focus on it. It's like buying a new car and suddenly realizing how many people drive that same model. It's all you can see."

"I suppose you're right."

"Are you okay, pet?" I let it slip. I shouldn't have called her that.

"No, but I will be now that you're here. You make things better."

I understand how she feels for once. Human emotions are complex, and while I understand them, they are also fairly new experiences for me. I've never felt them with this level of strength and veracity. It all changed when I laid eyes on her. The closer I am to her, and the longer I am near her, the stronger they feel.

She leans in to kiss me before pulling back to let me look at her. The last light from the day continues to recede, but it casts a beautiful shadow on her skin. I bring a hand to her cheek and caress it lightly.

"What happened?" I ask.

"I went home and found my ex banging my friend," she states coldly.

I freeze, not expecting her to say something so obscene. "You what?"

"That's not even the bad part. He made a comment about these." Her eyes turn downcast, insinuating that he was commenting on her scars.

"What the fuck did he say to you?" I can't help but let the anger exude from me. I want to hurt him. I want to torture him slowly until he can no longer breathe. I want him to feel endless pain and despair.

"He told me I was welcome to watch him fuck her and that it would give me a reason to cut myself." A tear falls from one of her eyes, and I wipe it away. "He then told me that the blades were on the sink waiting for me. I don't get it. Why does he have to be so cruel?"

"That must be his purpose," I mutter. The fucking audacity of this guy. I want to fix everything for her. I want to ensure he never speaks to her again, all while comforting her in the process.

"His purpose?" she questions.

Fuck. I didn't realize I said that out loud. "Yeah, some people are put in other people's lives to make them feel bad about things. He doesn't deserve any of your thoughts, Lena."

"Thank you for always listening when I need you." She smiles slightly, and a piece of me calms at the sight of happiness on her face. An idea pops into my head.

"What do you say we give Carson a little taste of his own medicine?" I know this is a bad idea, but I can't help but want to help her get back at him for what she had to witness today.

"What do you mean?"

"Take me home with you," I say.

"You want to go back to my apartment?" She gasps, but the idea intrigues her.

Having her go back there is not ideal. If there were any other options, I would choose them over this, but I'm limited here. Going with her is the best I can do in a place where I don't have a home of my own. I've never needed one. I am everywhere and nowhere at the same time. I've never desired to take a moment to rest.

"I'm not about to let you go back there alone, and it's too cold out here for us to stay outside. I would love to go to your apartment if you'll have me. Nothing has to happen that you don't want to."

I stand up and reach out my hand to her, prompting her to take it. She hesitates, glancing around for a moment before a mischievous grin crosses her face, and she places her hand in mine.

I lead her to her car and have her get in to warm up while I pick up the blanket and the miscellaneous items she used to cut herself with. If it's up to me, she will never feel the urge to cut again. However, if she does, I won't judge her.

After throwing everything in the car, I slip into the passenger seat and glance over at her. "Ready?"

"Didn't you drive here? What about your car?"

I didn't really think this through. I should have known she would ask about how I just magically showed up where she was. "You can just drop me off tomorrow, and I'll grab it then."

"Tomorrow? You're assuming I'm going to let you spend the night." She smirks and bats her lashes at me. She's in the mood to play, and I'm more than willing to oblige.

"I think you might consider it," I say while leaning in to kiss her neck. She turns her head further to the side, granting me more access and moans. Instantly, my cock hardens at the sound.

When I pull back, I see the way her chest heaves up and down, and her eyes are full of lust. She takes one steadying breath and drives us out of the cemetery. It doesn't take us long to arrive at her apartment building. When she parks the car in her usual parking spot, I sense the hesitation oozing from her.

"I'm right here by your side," I reassure her.

"Kellan, what are we? I know guys don't like to answer that question, but if I'm going to do this with you, I need to know what we are."

"You are mine," is all I say. It's the only thing that is true. Lena is mine. Every broken piece of her belongs to me.

Her eyes bounce back and forth between mine as if she's waiting for me to change my mind, but that will never happen. "Okay," she says with a sigh.

She pushes the car door open, and I follow suit. She stops next to me, and I reach out to hold her hand. When her fingers interlock with mine, every doubt she seems to have is replaced with nothing but pure confidence.

Her head is held high as she leads us into the building and right to the front door of her apartment. She slides the key in cautiously before pushing the door open. Carson is sitting on the couch directly across from us with a girl I recognize as Lexi. I know everyone Lena has interacted with in her time at Thorn Grove. Both Lexi and Carson sit in silence as Lena slowly closes the door behind us.

"I thought you would realize you're not wanted here," Carson snarls in her direction.

She shrinks into me, trying not to let his words affect her. I take a step forward, locking eyes with the piece of shit. "Talk to her like that again, and I'll rip out your tongue." I don't mean to be so aggressive about it, but his disrespect toward her brings out a side of me I didn't know I had.

I glance down to make sure I didn't freak her out, but she is smiling up at me. Her head whips back in their direction, and her posture is filled with the familiar confidence she had before walking into the apartment.

"This is Kellan, my boyfriend. You're welcome to watch if you want." She reaches up to grab the back of my neck and pulls me into a kiss. I comply, letting her take the lead. She deepens it further, brushing her tongue against mine and nipping at my bottom lip before pulling back.

Carson and Lexi stand up to storm past us toward the door. I hear him mutter "slut" under his breath, and I see red. He's done talking to her like that. Just before he gets out of the door, I reach out to grab his hair with my fingers. I rip him backward, making him fall to the floor before leaning down and laying blow after blow into his smug face. I hear a cracking noise that makes me smile when my fist connects with his nose.

"Kellan, stop. He's not worth it," Lena calls out, her voice pulling me from my angry abyss.

I step away from him, admiring the way the blood drips from his nose. He's lucky he will only have a bloody nose and a black eye.

"Get the fuck out, and if you ever talk to her like that again, I want you to remember this moment," I seethe.

He doesn't say anything at all. He just scurries away like the cockroach he is. As soon as the door slams shut, Lena jumps into my arms, wrapping her legs around my waist. I catch her, holding her up by the bottom of her thighs. Her lips land on mine, and I groan at the contact. She runs her fingers through my hair with one hand as the other sits along the base of my neck. I take a few steps forward, trying to find somewhere for us to land.

She pulls back for a moment, panting, and points me in the direction of her bedroom. Once inside, I drop her down on the edge of the bed and sink to my knees in front of her. My hands reach out to grip the waistband of her leggings and panties, and she tilts her hips up, allowing me to pull them off.

I grip the backs of her knees and pull forward. Her back falls to the bed, and I place myself between her legs. I lean down and pepper kisses up the length of each one of them, wanting to savor every single piece of her. She props herself up on her elbows with her gaze focused solely on me.

My nose trails along her center, and I can smell her arousal as she bucks her hips from the slight contact. Her breath hitches when I lean to kiss the sensitive area near the apex of her thighs.

"Kellan," she pants.

"Yes, pet."

"Make me feel good."

A sly smile crosses my face. I throw her legs over my shoulders and claim my prize. I run my tongue along her opening, savoring the taste of her before flicking her clit. I tasted her in her dreams, but nothing compares to real life.

She moans before lacing her fingers in my hair. With a soft tug, she positions me right where she wants me. I twirl my tongue all around her clit, relishing in the subtle way her body writhes beneath me.

"Kellan, more please," she begs.

Who am I to say no? Slowly, I slide two fingers inside her and pump them in and out until I find the perfect spot that makes her sing for me. I focus my fingers on that, thrusting them in and out of her wet pussy as I suck on her clit.

I free my mouth from her to test the waters biting down on her inner thigh. "Fuckkkk," she whines.

"A perfect slut for me," I praise, her eyes lighting up with desire.

"Yes," she breathes, not taking those beautiful browns off of me.

I dive back into her pussy with a renewed passion, believing she can handle anything I dole out to her. I add a third finger and focus my attention back on her clit, feeling the way her pussy spasms with each flick of my tongue.

She's close already, and it makes anticipation run through my veins. I can't wait to see the look on her face and feel the way her body falls apart because of me outside of her dreams. I pick up my pace, and her hips buck in response.

"Come for me, pet. Soak my fingers like a good little whore."

I lean back in, sucking on her clit to give her the last little push she needs, and she does exactly what I told her to. She grinds her pussy all over my face, finding pure bliss. I'm transfixed by the furrow in her brow and the way her mouth has transformed into the perfect 'O' shape.

"Oh my God!" she cries out.

"Not God, but not the Devil either." I chuckle to myself as my fingers continue their pace, letting her ride out her high.

When her hand falls from my hair, I pull back to quickly strip out of my clothes. I'm not done with her yet. She glances down at my fully erect cock, and she takes in a sharp breath. She follows suit and strips her top half bare before positioning herself in the center of the bed. I climb on top of her, wasting no time placing myself back between her legs.

My mouth lands on her neck, biting and sucking up the length of it. She may have marks there in the morning, and the idea sends a thrill through me. I grind my cock along her center, and she leans into it. She likes things dirty, so it's time to spice things up a notch. I reach my hand out and wrap it around her delicate little throat. Her eyes glimmer in delight as I begin to squeeze.

"How badly do you want me to fuck you, pet? Will you beg for it?" I know I'm pushing it a bit with the number of times I've called her pet, but I can't stop. "Beg me to fuck you like the desperate slut you are."

"Please, fuck me."

"You can do better than that," I tell her, tightening my grip on her throat and grinding my cock on her sensitive clit.

"Fuck me like a dirty whore, please," she begs. The moment those words leave her lips, I lose control.

I release my grip on her neck, flip her over so that she's on her hands and knees, and pull her ass toward me. "Face down on the bed. Be a good girl," I say as I push between her shoulder blades. She doesn't hesitate to comply, keeping her ass perched up in the air for me and pressing her face to the sheets.

I grip her hips and line myself up, taking a moment to admire her glistening pussy, before slamming into her with one brutal thrust. She gasps at my intrusion, and I relish the way she stretches around my cock. She feels so fucking good. I've thought about this very moment over and over, and it's even more amazing than I could have imagined.

"So fucking tight and so wet just for me." I thrust into her, loving the way her pussy spasms every time I rock my hips.

"Yes, it's all for you," she moans.

I pick up my pace and bring a hand down to slap one of her ass cheeks, making her cry out. Slowly, I rub the area that has already started to redden while continuing to pump my cock in and out. I repeat the process a few more times, loving the way she cries out with every smack.

"More please," she whines.

I pull out of her for just a moment to shove my fingers inside her pussy to get them nice and wet before sliding them up to her ass.

"Dirty slut needs more?" I ask

"Yes," she breathes out.

Without another word, I shove my cock back inside her pussy and slowly push a finger into her ass. Her head tilts back as the mixture of pleasure and pain overwhelms her. She needs to get used to all of her holes being filled. My shadow has a mind of its own sometimes, and once I am able to fuck her in my true form, I will definitely be using every glorious part of her entire body.

I reach around with my free hand to rub on her clit, stimulating as many parts of her at one time as I can in this form. She moans, getting close to exactly where I want her. I won't come without her coating my cock again. I may be Death, but I'm a gentleman.

"I love when your cunt squeezes me like that. Give me more, pet. Give me all of you and come for me."

I pick up my relentless pace fucking her pretty pussy with my cock and thrusting my finger in her ass. I add slightly more pressure to her clit, and she pushes her ass back to meet my thrusts. It gives her the extra stimulation she needs to find her release.

She cries out, clamping down on me, and my balls tighten. The sweet sound of her pleasure is something I could listen to on repeat. Her eyes squeeze shut, and she grips the sheets to ride out her orgasm. I don't dare let up or change my pace even the slightest bit. Instead, I come with her, shooting every drop of my essence inside her perfect pussy.

"That's my perfect girl," I say before pulling out and falling onto the bed next to her. I turn her to face me and pull her close.

"We didn't use a condom." She sighs. "That was reckless. I always try to be safe."

"You don't have to worry, Lena. I would never risk your safety," I reassure her. I want to tell her that I can't contract human diseases, but that would just lead to more questions. I just leave it with this for now, "I can't produce children if you're worried about that."

She gasps like she wasn't expecting that kind of admission from me but lowers her gaze a bit in disappointment. "Neither can I."

I tilt her head up and steal her thoughts by planting a kiss on her lips. "That's okay. You're never going to be alone again." Her eyes sparkle with something I can't quite name as I promise to be by her side through anything. She is mine, and I meant that when I claimed her. "Let's get you cleaned up."

I stand up and lead her to the bathroom, making sure to turn on the warm water before ushering her under it and stepping in behind her. The first thing I grab is her shampoo. I squirt some of the citrus-scented liquid into my hand and lather it into her hair. Her head falls back on my chest as she lets out a relieved sigh.

After a moment, she pulls her head up, and I help her rinse soapy bubbles from her hair. I repeat the same process with her conditioner before grabbing her loofah and sliding it along her entire body. Once she's clean, she turns to face me and wraps her arms around my waist. I bring my arms around her, and we stand there for a moment, letting the warm water embrace us as though we are one.

"Let's get to bed, pet." I lean down to shut off the water.

She wraps a towel around her body and reaches out to hand me one. "Only if you come with me." A soft blush flushes her cheeks, and I smile at her.

"There's nowhere else I would rather be."

We walk hand in hand to her bedroom before I let go of her to secure the door shut, locking it behind me. I lean down to grab the boxers I had on before and slide them up my waist, watching her as she opens one of her dresser drawers to pull out an oversized shirt and a pair of panties.

After dressing, she snuggles under the covers, letting me slide in next to her. I pull her against my body and hold her tightly until she falls asleep in my arms. She looks so peaceful. It's almost like she's a different person from the one who spends so much of her day struggling to simply be alive.

I lean in and kiss her lightly on the forehead before carefully untangling myself from her hold. I have a few souls that have been calling out. I'll just slip away for a short while to handle business and return to my girl's arms as though I never left.

Before I fade away to collect the first soul, two figures appear in front of me, and I know my uninterrupted time with Lena is up.

Chapter 11

Kellan

I 've been expecting The Others to send their little minions after me but doing it immediately after I shared such a special moment with my pet has me annoyed at their presence. The two of them prompt me to take us to a location where we can have a more private conversation, so I bring us to the cemetery. I find it all too fitting that this was the first place I truly defied their masters.

I eye them with annoyance as they take their stance in front of me. "Angel, demon, care to tell me why you're interrupting my duties? I have souls to collect."

The demon chuckles at my attempt to be coy. "Don't play stupid with us, reaper. You know why we're here. You couldn't resist getting your dick wet, so we were sent to warn you."

The angel looks over at me, sympathy filling their eyes. "It's forbidden. Death is not supposed to find companionship in the souls he leads."

"I am aware of what is expected of me," I tell them.

"You are to be neutral. You are not to interfere with a soul's purpose. Inserting yourself into her path could potentially lead to her eternal damnation," the angel tries to tell me.

"Me inserting myself into her path will not lead anywhere because she is staying with me."

"You can't be serious." The demon raises a brow at me. "You truly think you'll get to keep her? That's not how this works, and you know that. She will end up with one of us, and you'll go back to carrying out your pathetic existence alone."

"There is balance for a reason," the angel tries to argue.

"I don't give a fuck about balance anymore. Tell your God and Devil that Lena is mine. I won't allow either of you to take her from me."

"This will have further repercussions if you continue down this path," the angel tells me, their eyes full of concern.

The demon takes a step toward me. "You didn't actually catch feelings for this human, did you? Death with feelings? I didn't think you were even capable of real emotions."

"That's enough," the angel tells him before looking back at me. "If you insist on continuing with your decision, there will be serious consequences. Consider this your warning."

"Heard, loud and clear, but I'm not going to stop. You two run back and tell The Others they need to make an exception. You preach of balance, correct? Even Death deserves a companion. That is balance."

They look at me quizzically before glancing back at one another and disappearing without any further conversation. That went about as well as it could have.

I've been assertive with my intentions, and I don't plan on budging. My only hope is that they are considered. Lena is mine.

She is not going anywhere. They will have to pry her out of my cold, dead hands first.

Fuck their rules. I won't keep lying to her anymore, at least not about who I really am. I've been nervous about how receptive she would be and what consequences may come from it. What it really comes down to is if I'm willing to risk everything for her, I need to make sure I am even something she would want.

I'm not sure how to tell her about my realm or her connection to me and it. I suppose I will start by showing her my true form before diving deeper into the technicalities of everything else.

A familiar sound rings in my ears. I need to get some work in. Having those unexpected visitors put me behind, and I have a whole list of souls to collect before getting back to my girl. I'm hoping to get there before she wakes up in the morning. I don't want her to think I've slipped out in the night like I'm ashamed to be with her. Then, I will tell her everything bit by bit.

Most of the souls I encountered tonight didn't give me any issues. I popped in, they grabbed my hand for comfort or walked alongside me, and we moved on. This last soul is proving to be a bit difficult. It's a middle-aged man who appears to be clinging to something near his hospital bed.

A woman sits next to the bed with tears running down her face. She is gripping onto his hand as if it would end her to let him go. She is screaming as people run into the room to try and revive him. His time is up, and I have appeared to collect him, but he refuses to come with me.

His soul moves around the room in an attempt to comfort the woman who seems distraught over the possibility of losing him. Before I interacted with Lena, this scene wouldn't have affected me, but I find myself feeling sympathy for the two of them. I find myself hesitating to try and give the doctors a few extra moments to reconnect his soul to his body.

"We must go," I say. I never speak to them, but for some reason, I want to comfort him.

"I can't leave her yet," he says, as the doctors place a machine on his chest and his body surges upward.

She screams from the corner of the room, and again, I hesitate. This isn't like me at all. Lena changed the way I see the parting of two lovers, so I grant him more time. His body jolts on the bed again, and his soul reunites with it. Just like that, his clock is reset, and it is no longer his time.

When his eyes open in his body, he looks to the corner of the room where I stand and mouths, "Thank you," as if I did it intentionally. I stand there watching for a moment, his eyes never leaving mine as his wife leaps toward him, grateful he is still alive. I feel a twinge in my chest and understand fully what love is in this moment. Because he saw my true form and I didn't take him, he will be tethered to me until we meet again. Surprisingly, I'm okay with that. I nod at him and disappear in a smoky haze.

Now that my work is caught up, I reappear in the bathroom of her apartment in an attempt to keep her from seeing me right away. A gasp from the corner of the room has me turning, face to face, with the girl who has my entire being in a chokehold.

She sits there on the toilet, frozen in place, her eyes as wide as saucers. She blinks a few times, shaking her head, and then locks her eyes back on me. She takes in the entirety of my form, glancing first at the shadowy tendrils that float in the smoky air along my lower half. Her eyes trail up higher to my cloaked center and then to each of my shadowy arms with tendrils spiraling from them.

When her gaze lands on my green eyes, she pauses. Her brows furrow and she tilts her head to the side, almost as though she recognizes me. No, there is no way she would be able to discern that.

After wiping, she stands from the toilet, pulls up her panties, and turns to flush it before walking to the sink to wash her hands. She glances over her shoulder at me again to see if I am still there but doesn't appear to be frightened. She simply goes on with completing her task.

I've never had a human react to me like this. Generally, they emit some sort of fear or concern in my presence. It is not normal for someone to be so comfortable around death. Their instincts tell them they should be anxious even at the idea of me.

She grabs the towel hanging next to the sink to dry her hands and then turns to face me. Again, her eyes meet mine, and they are filled with curiosity. She takes a step toward me, and I find myself riddled with anxiety. With every movement of her closing the distance between us, the anticipation only grows.

Finally, she stops in front of me, staring directly into my eyes, and places a hand on my shadow form. The smoke billows out around her hand before enveloping it. She watches as her hand disappears into the darkness of my being. I can tell she is confused over being able to press her skin against me but still having the shadowy smoke floating around it.

She closes her eyes for a moment, just feeling where our bodies connect. I am still standing here frozen, unsure of what to do. I intended to show her my shadow form, but it was after I had spoken to her. I didn't want it to happen this way, with her unprepared. I suppose I could dissipate. I could leave her here to question if what she saw was real, but that would only delay the inevitable.

My tendrils float around her body, pulling her closer to me. Her touching me in my true form has only intensified the way I feel for her. She glances down at the tendril on her hip, and her breath hitches.

I lock eyes with her again, watching the way she is studying me. Why is she not afraid? Does she know what death means? Does she understand the finality of it all? Is she hoping that I will take her and bring her peace? I am completely taken aback by her reaction, so much so that I just continue to stand there like a fool.

"Kellan?" she questions, and I almost burst at the seams. It takes everything in me to register that I'm not imagining it.

Chapter 12

Lena

I would recognize his eyes anywhere. The sparkling green hues draw me in and evoke nothing but peace. They are the only eyes I've looked into that did not feel like they were expecting something from me. I should be terrified, but I only feel comfort and a sense of calm. The strange pull I've always felt toward him feels so much stronger right now with him like this.

"Kellan?" I question, but still, he just stands there, looking at me as if I am a ghost.

I think he may be more affected by this entire scenario than I am, which I find amusing. I'm confused, sure, but I know he would never hurt me. He seems thoroughly traumatized right now based on the way his eyes refuse to leave mine.

"Kellan?" I ask again, waiting for him to confirm my suspicions, but he remains silent.

I wrap my arms around his midsection, surprised by how solid he seems, considering, to the blind eye, he appears more like a floating cloud of smoke and shadows. I pull him in for a hug, resting my face on his cloaked midsection. Chills spread across my body from the close contact, and I've never felt so sure

I belong somewhere until right now. I know with full certainty that I belong in his arms.

"I know it's you," I tell him as dark shadows surround the parts of me that touch him. "I need you to talk to me and tell me what's going on."

I stay here like this for a moment, feeling his feathery touch all around me. I take a deep breath, taking in his scent, and it reminds me of a warm summer day after it rains, fresh and clean. When he still doesn't say anything, I release my hold and step back to look at him. His refusal to speak is extremely frustrating.

"Are you going to talk to me, damn it? I know it's you. Speak up and tell me what the fuck is going on, so I don't have to try and work this out for myself."

He turns his head to the side in confusion. "Why aren't you trying to escape me?"

"Why would I? You haven't done anything?"

"Lena, most humans who are not on their immediate deathbed have some sort of response to the sight of me: fear, anxiety, anticipation, something. The feelings I sense from you right now are peace, curiosity, and tranquility. I don't understand." His voice is deeper than I've heard it sound before.

"So, you're admitting it is you? I guess I don't have to take you back to your car at the graveyard then. Do you even have a car?"

"You're not focusing on the correct questions."

"The only question I'm focused on at the moment is whether or not my new boyfriend is the shadowy figure standing in front of me. If you could confirm, that would be fantastic." I can tell he is irritated with me, but I don't care.

A moment later, the shadowy figure vanishes, and the very handsome man I've been spending my time with appears in its place.

"Yes. I am one and the same," he confirms. "Do you not have other questions?"

"Is this a dream? I hope I'm not sleeping because if I am, then I should be concerned with how active my imagination is." I pinch my arm, and it hurts. I must be awake.

"You're not sleeping."

"Okay." I grab his hand and pull him back toward my bedroom. I don't want to be talking about this in the open, in case captain douchebag and my ex-friend decide to come back to the apartment.

Once we are inside my room, I lock the door and turn to face him. He is seated on the edge of the bed, wearing nothing besides a pair of shorts. The light that shines around him from the early morning sun makes me want to jump on top of him and have a repeat of last night. The tattoos around his arms seem brighter than usual; the black roses and smokey tendrils have a new meaning now.

"Lena," he warns, as though he can somehow sense my thoughts.

"Can you read my mind?" I ask, laughing at the words that just poured out of my mouth. Of all the questions I could ask, this is the first one. I bite my lip and glance toward the outline of his cock in his shorts.

"No, I cannot read your mind. I can sense your emotions. I can also see the way you're rubbing your thighs together. We have things to discuss."

He's right. I have to get serious. I ask the question that should have been the first thing out of my mouth when I saw his shadow figure in my bathroom. "What are you?"

"I am Death."

His answer is simple and yet complicated. "You're Death?"

"Yes, I am the harbinger of death. Many know me as The Grim Reaper."

"If you're real, what about God and the Devil, angels, demons, vampires? Are fucking vampires real? Oh my god! Are mermaids real?" I feel a little bit like I'm on the verge of spiraling out of control, but when I look at him, I instantly feel calm again.

"God and the Devil, yes, although I prefer to refer to them as The Others. Angels and demons, also yes. They're annoying little fuckers too. Vampires and mermaids are definitely not real." He chuckles at the last one as though it's the craziest thing he's ever heard. Almost as crazy as him being the Grim Reaper. "You should know there are rules, and The Others will not be happy about you discovering my true form and linking it to my human one."

"What will happen?" I inquire.

"I'm not sure, but it will most likely not be good. We will have to wait and see."

That sounds oddly ominous, and I'm not sure I like it. I want to ask him other questions, but a sudden realization shocks me to my core.

"Let me get this straight, last night, I fucked Death?" I can't help the laugh that bursts from me. It seems like the most ridiculous thing I've ever heard, and yet, he is standing right in front of me. I have to be sleeping. There is no way this is real life right now. I can't stop laughing.

"Yes, that would be correct."

"I'm alive, though. I don't understand. You have a human form but also a shadow form?"

"I have magic that grants me the ability to appear as though I am human. It is necessary due to the potential interactions I have with the souls I collect. My job is to lead them to my realm once their time in their human life has expired so that they can carry out their purpose. I watch and never get involved."

"Clearly you got involved with me."

"I did. Are you afraid of me now?"

"No, I'm not afraid, Kellan. I told you already. I feel comfortable around you. You make me feel safe." I shake my head and walk over to sit on the bed next to him. "Did I see you the day I tried to kill myself in my bathroom? I thought I was going crazy or hallucinating."

"Yes, it was the first time I laid eyes on you. I haven't been able to get you off my mind or stay away from you since that day. You have become somewhat of an obsession for me."

"I don't understand. How can Death be obsessed with someone, and why would it be me? I'm nobody."

He reaches over to grip my chin, forcing me to look at him. "You are everything, pet."

Pet. The name that he called me last night while we were intimate. I almost didn't connect the two pieces, but they are all falling together now. I thought I imagined his shadow form before. I dreamt he was fucking me with it. There was also the time I saw him in the corner of the room while I was getting myself off. How many other times has he been lurking around without me knowing?

"Pet? You've called me that before." I want to see if he is going to lie to me. If he can pick up on feelings, then he must know I've connected the dots. My mind can rationalize my boyfriend being a shadowy figure of death, but lying is where I cross the line, apparently. Yet another reason why I am truly fucked up in the head.

"I did. Last night," he tries.

"No, I've heard you call me that before last night."

He studies me for a moment before he nods. "In your dream."

"Was that real?"

"Yes, and no. I was not physically there with you, but my conscious mind was active in it. I felt the same experiences as you. You were the one to imagine me there. The thoughts were all yours until I manipulated them a bit. You were impossible to resist. I had to feel your sweet cunt even if it wasn't physically happening." My cheeks heat at his confession. His hand trails down my neck, and goosebumps follow the path in his wake. He rests his hand on my thigh, and my eyes focus on the contact.

"I saw your shadow form another time, too," I admit.

"That's not possible. The only times I've shown my true form to you was in your dream, accidentally today, and when you were bleeding out on your bathroom floor."

"You were hiding in the corner of my old bedroom. I didn't realize it was you at the time because I didn't get a clear look. I only saw shadows." I think back to when I saw the figure watch me get myself off.

His body visibly stiffens. "You saw a dark shadowy figure, yet you continued to pleasure yourself? Do you have no self-preservation at all?"

"You don't have to be an asshole. I didn't feel threatened, and I wanted to come. It's that simple. If I die, I die. I don't fear death, Kellan. I've been skirting it my entire life."

"You are so different from any of the other souls I've ever encountered."

"Is that a bad thing?"

"Not for me, but for you, maybe. You should, at the very least, be apprehensive of me. I am Death, Lena. I have been watching you, stalking you, for over two years."

"Is that so?" I decide to be bold and stand up to pull my shirt over my head before letting my panties drop to the ground and stepping out of them one foot at a time.

"You are such a curious thing." His eyes roam my naked body, making me blush. I can tell by the way he says it that he is consumed with nothing but thoughts of me.

"I get it now."

"Get what?" he asks.

"The reason I'm so comfortable around you. I've been craving you for so long. I've lived a shell of a life. When I'm around you, it's like I can breathe for the first time in years. All the fatigue and worthlessness I'm usually wrought with disappears with the slightest touch from you. I'm drawn to you and the peace you bring me."

"We are both drawn to one another then." He pulls me onto his lap. My legs straddle either side of him, and I can feel him harden in his shorts beneath me, his cock pressed up against my center. I do my best to resist grinding on him.

"When I'm near you, I feel normal, happy."

He grabs me by the back of the neck and crashes his mouth onto mine. The moment our lips touch, everything in me ignites. My lips part with a gasp, and his tongue slips between them.

When he pulls back, he stares directly into my soul. "When I am near you, every single fiber of my being comes to life. You bring life to death."

My eyes widen, and my eyebrows rise as I try to process exactly what he just said. I bring life to death. Me? The basic girl from Cherry Hill, with black hair, pale skin, and brown eyes, brings life to death? I look more like death than anything.

"Don't doubt yourself, pet."

"I like it when you call me that." I lean forward and rest my forehead on his, our lips so close to one another I can feel the vibrations radiating from him.

"You do?" he asks while trailing a hand up my back, giving me goosebumps. His touch is almost too much for me to handle.

"Yes," I breathe out.

"My dirty girl. You want me to fuck you, don't you?" He pushes his cock up to grind against my soaking center. "You want me to slide my cock into your tight little pussy?"

"Mmmm, that sounds nice."

He shifts into his shadow form under me. "What if I took you like this? I could fuck you like I did in your dream. Would a filthy slut like you enjoy that?"

"Fuck yes, I would," I tell him, grinding my pussy against his lap. I pause for a moment and pull back to look at him. "Is it the same for you? Do you feel the same sensations in this form as your human one?"

He grabs me and flips us around. My back is now on the mattress, and one of his shadowy tendrils holds my arms above my head. My feet are pulled to either side of the bed. Something grips at each one of my ankles, keeping me spread wide for him.

He looms over me with those perfect green eyes that look right into the depths of my soul.

"It feels so much more intense to touch you in my natural form. Forbidden. Exciting. It's like every part of you devours even the smallest part of me. I'm fucking addicted to the feeling."

I feel it, too. Having his shadows all around me makes my body practically weep for him to touch me.

"Fuck me then," I beg, trying to pull myself forward to kiss him but he's just out of reach, and I grow frustrated.

"Are you sure you realize what you're asking me?" He seems to hesitate, but I am so turned on I think I would combust if he left me here like this.

"Fuck me, Kellan. And don't be gentle. Show me what it's like to belong to Death."

Chapter 13

Kellan

I almost can't contain my shadow when she asks me to fuck her. I had no idea this was where the early morning would take us, but you won't find me complaining. She is absolutely perfect for me in every way. She isn't afraid of me or what I represent. She only embraces every part of it.

"When I take you in this form, you will be mine forever. I'll make sure of it. You were going to be anyway, but if you choose to have me like this, you'll never be free of me again. You're positive that's what you want?"

"Yes. I'll choose you every day if you need me to."

I lean in. "Greedy girl. We'll see how confident you are when my shadow fills all your holes like a filthy whore. Maybe I should play with you for hours until you beg me to let you come."

"Please," she groans, and it's the sweetest sound.

"Next time, pet. I've been waiting too long to have you like this to have any kind of restraint today. Let me see that pretty pussy."

My shadows pull at all her limbs, spreading her legs wider. I can see her dripping cunt and I know it's all for me. I concentrate my smoky mass and form a phantom hand before running a finger across her deliciously wet center.

She moans, "More."

"So eager to be a perfect slut for me."

I push two shadowy fingers inside her, and she clamps down around them instantly. She takes them so well, like she was made for me. I push in and out of her at a painfully slow pace, building her up just enough to push her to the edge but not enough to let her fall over it. I may be eager to be inside her, but I still want to tease her a bit. She's so much more beautiful when she's desperate and begging. Her chest rises and falls, and I can feel her heart slamming in her chest.

"Kellan," she begs, and I smile at her. "Kellan, please."

Hearing her say my name will never get old. I pull my shadow fingers from her and place my form between her beautiful thighs. A tendril reaches out and wraps itself around her delicate throat, applying the perfect amount of pressure.

"Look at you, so desperate to be a whore for Death."

I line myself up and slowly slide inside her. Her back arches up off the bed as her pussy stretches around my shadow cock. She gasps, probably wanting to tell me that it's too much, but with my tendril wrapped around her throat, she's not able to speak.

"You're taking me so well, pet. Breathe," I instruct her, loosening my grip on her throat. She listens and takes a deep breath.

I lean into her, watching as goosebumps appear everywhere our bodies touch. A tendril finds its way to her clit, rubbing small circles as I begin to thrust inside her. She moans loudly as her pleasure builds. The only thing I want to see is the look on her face as she comes for me in my true form.

I've learned the more I degrade her, the more her body ignites, so I've been trying to incorporate it in more. These aren't words I've ever said in this way before, but I love the way she reacts to them. Her nipples pebble, and her pussy clenches every time I call her my slut.

"Does my filthy slut want to come?"

"Yes," she moans and clenches around me again, exactly how I want her to.

"Do it. Show me how desperate you are to belong to me. Come on my cock, pet."

She falls over the edge on command, crying out my name as her warm release heats my shadow. I continue thrusting in and out while her pussy flutters around me. As she begins to come down, I decide I'm nowhere near done with her. I want to hear her moans on repeat.

My shadow tightens around her throat again, ready to take this up to another level. I pull my cock out, and her juices drip down to her tight hole. I bring another shadowy extension of myself out to spread it around. She is at my mercy, and I promised to fill all her holes. I quickly shove my cock back inside her pussy, as the shadow extension massages its way into her ass. Just like in her dream, she has me filling her in both places at the same time.

"That's two holes filled now. Sluts get them all filled, don't they?" I ask, releasing the grip on her throat as I thrust in and out of her.

"It's so much," she says as a tear slips from the corner of her eye and falls down her cheek. I never thought I would enjoy seeing her cry but having her at my mercy is a fucking gorgeous sight.

"Who do you belong to?" I ask, already knowing the answer but I want to hear it directly from her.

"You," she moans, "I belong to you, always."

"Fuck yes, you do, pet. You're mine, and you'll never leave me. I won't allow it."

I slam my cock along her sensitive walls, making her cry out. My shadow tendril that was wrapped around her throat, takes the opportunity to fill her parted mouth. It presses down on her tongue, forcing her to keep it open.

Drool seeps from the sides of her mouth, and her nostrils flare. She loves every moment of this. When I reach out and pinch one of her nipples her eyes roll back in pleasure, so I repeat the process on the other side. I feel my release building inside me, my shadow threatening to explode, but I want her to ride out that high with me.

"Come again like a good little slut," I tell her before tweaking her nipple again.

She tightens around my cock, and I can feel the electricity bouncing between her body and mine. Her back arches, and her eyes squeeze shut as she succumbs to the pleasure. I come with her, shooting the cool release of my shadow inside her. She twitches at the sensation.

I shift back into my human form to pull her in close. She snuggles into my chest and fits perfectly. It's as though she's always belonged there.

"You're perfect," I whisper in her ear, trying to steady my breathing. Being like this with her is more than I could have ever imagined.

"That was..." She trails off, eyes full of emotion, before a huge smile consumes the entirety of her face. She bursts out into a fit of laughter, and I'm immediately confused. How can she go from being so serious to borderline hysteria?

"Are you okay?"

"I just willingly fucked Death," she says before she starts laughing again.

"I'm a bit confused. Is that a bad thing?"

She reaches up to touch my face, and I lean into it. "No, it's not a bad thing. I'm just having a moment. Life has been fucking me for years, and I just find it super ironic that I fucked Death."

"You can do it again if it will keep making you laugh like that." I trail my finger along her shoulder down her arm. I love hearing her laugh. Usually, she carries around such a painful aura.

"We will absolutely be doing that again. I have to get ready for class, though." She sighs.

Just tell her. I think to myself, but I can't. The Others will already be angry enough at me. I don't want them to think she will keep me from performing my duties. With any luck, they will see that I can have her, and nothing will change.

"I suppose you're right. I have work to do anyway."

"Work?" She questions.

"Yes. As you know, I am the harbinger of death. I have to lead the souls to my realm."

She takes a moment to absorb my words. "What's it like, always seeing the end of someone's life?"

"It's always different. It all depends on the circumstances surrounding the end of their human lives."

"But you never get to see any of the good parts."

I never thought about it like that. I've spent so long being focused on my job and ensuring the souls are on their correct path that I never cared about what their lives were like or the things they did prior to meeting them. Even now, I still don't care about them. The only one that matters to me is her—the brown-eyed beauty lying next to me.

I run my hand along her cheek. "Lena, you are the only soul that means anything to me. Nobody else matters. It's only you."

"What's so special about me?"

"When I'm in your presence, I come alive."

"It's like you can finally breathe," she whispers as a tear slips from the corner of her eye.

I nod before leaning in to kiss her softly. "I really should get going so I can get back to you. If you're ever in need, call out my name. As long as I'm able to, I will come for you."

I stand and shift back into my true form to escort the first soul, but before I leave, she calls out to me.

"Kellan."

I turn to look at her. "Yes, pet?"

"I'm yours."

I shift back to my human self and lunge toward her, pressing my lips against hers again. She is mine—mine—and I will never let her go. I pull back, and she wraps her arms around me one last time before letting me free.

"You're mine," I confirm before shifting and disappearing to collect my first soul of the day.

It's an older man who is sitting in his car. His death was sudden, a heart attack. I walk up to him, wondering if he has any loved ones that he's leaving behind. He catches sight of me, and a sense of understanding washes over him. I reach out, and he grabs my hand. In a flash, we vanish. I bring him to my realm and urge him off to continue his purpose.

I'm about to move on to collect the next soul when two familiar figures appear in front of me. The angel and demon. This can't be good. I grow anxious over the possible consequences they are here to advise me of. The Others sending them means they know I didn't heed their warning.

"You broke the rules, Death," the demon says with a smile on his face, getting right to the point.

"I didn't break the rules. I didn't intentionally show her my true shadow form outside of her dream world. We all know that dreams are a gray area." I walk forward to stand closer to the angel because, quite frankly, the demon is pissing me off. "Don't get me wrong, I planned to tell her. She just beat me to it. She accidentally saw my shadow form when I appeared in her bathroom. She recognized my eyes."

"Yes, we are aware of the details of the encounter," The angel says. They give me a pitying smile.

"A technicality. You still placed yourself in her path. You are still the reason the incident occurred, and you changed her purpose. There are punishments for that," the demon huffs.

My breathing quickens, and I feel butterflies in the pit of my stomach. I changed her purpose. Could this mean she will be allowed to stay with me? I wait to see what the two of them have to say next. The Others must have a message for me.

"These are strange circumstances, Death. This has never happened throughout the expanse of time. God and the Devil have settled upon a fair solution, but you must agree to abide by it. If you do not agree, your access to her will be taken."

"They will do no such thing! Lena is mine!" I growl, smoke billowing all around me.

"If you wish for a chance at keeping her, you will agree to follow a few new rules for the time being," the angel sings out.

Time freezes and I have no other choice but to agree. I have a chance to keep her. My only hope is that these rules are achievable because there is no way I am letting anyone take her from me, not God or the Devil.

"What are your rules? I will follow them."

The two of them glance at one another to see who will tell me the news. Finally, the angel makes eye contact with me. "You are not to see her again until this plays out."

"You can't keep me away from her," I try, but the angel only shakes their head.

"These are the rules that have been selected. You will stay away from her for a short period of time in order for her to fulfill a new purpose and she will need to choose you. She will need to choose her life with you over the convenience of death. You are only being offered this because you have not confessed everything to her entirely. If she can withstand time without your presence and choose to live, then she will be given the choice to stay with you forever."

I mull over their words for a moment. Lena doesn't know what I know. I didn't get a chance to tell her everything. Now she is supposed to choose strength and life. She needs to choose life to be shackled to Death for all of eternity. She wants me. I know she does. Our connection, the pull the two of us feel for one another, is strong. I know it.

"This is the only way?"

"Yes, her existence has become incongruous. This is the only way to rectify that," the angel says with a sigh as if this is hard for them to talk about.

"Reaper, if you attempt to interfere again, we will take her from you," the demon says with his sadistic grin. "You should know, if she takes her life, her soul will belong to my master."

"The fuck it will! How do you expect me to sit back and watch her struggle, to watch her hurt? How long exactly am I supposed to stay on the sidelines?"

"For however long it takes. It could be a day; it could be a month. The timeline is up to her. Interfere or don't, it doesn't matter to me." The demon laughs.

"Kellan," the angel says firmly, pulling my attention back over to them. I used to crave being called by my true name rather than what I represent but it doesn't sound right coming from anyone besides my pet. She is the only one with the right to call me that.

"I wasn't aware we were on a true name basis." I glare at them.

"Give her a chance and have faith that all of this will work out the way you hope for."

"Fine. I'll stay away—for now." And I will because I believe them when they say this is her only chance. She needs to choose me. I have to trust our connection with one another.

"The plus side to not worrying about her is that you can get back to work uninterrupted," the demon remarks.

"Fuck off. Don't you two have somewhere else to be? I get it. I'll stay away. You can tell The Others I will stay in line. Now, leave," I hiss.

With that, they disappear, and I find myself wishing I had stayed with her longer than I did this morning. I should have confessed everything to her and told her that I love her. Who knows if I will be able to the next time I see her.

I'm forced into the shadows again. Compelled to watch her potentially suffer and do nothing to intervene. As much as the idea rips apart every fiber of my being, I have to do it. It's the only chance we have to be together. They gave us a chance, and I have to hold onto that.

Chapter 14

Lena

I've been alone for six days. I thought Kellan and I had something special, but after he slept with me in his shadow form, he never came back. I try calling out for him like he told me to, but it doesn't matter how many times I call his name. He never comes.

I wonder if it was all a lie. I don't want to believe that, but what else am I supposed to believe with him ghosting me? *Ghosting me.* I laugh. He's not technically a ghost, but it's still funny.

Was it all a ruse to get me to sleep with him? I don't suppose the Grim Reaper would have a huge need to be between someone's legs. His human form is hot enough he could pull in whoever he wanted, whenever he wanted.

What the fuck is wrong with me for thinking like this? How do I even know that part of the night was even real? I know Kellan, as a human, is real. We slept together and had our daily lunches between my classes. He took the time to get to know me. It would have been pointed out if I had been sitting in the dining hall talking to myself every day. They would have definitely made fun of me for it.

The people on this campus all seem to get some sort of sick pleasure out of making me their social target. I thought people grew out of this once they left high school, but I was definitely wrong there.

Was the second half of the night six days ago a dream? Maybe Kellan left after we had sex, and it was all in my head. I've dreamed about the shadows before.

No, fuck that. It was real. It had to be. It didn't feel anything like a dream.

I thought we had a connection, but he's been radio silent. What did I do wrong? Did he realize being with me as his true self wasn't what he expected? The thoughts have been spiraling in my head for almost a week now. I hate feeling so alone again. It's worse now because I experienced those peaceful moments with him. I know what it's like to have that, and losing it has me feeling so fucking empty.

I squeeze my books close to my chest and practically run to my class, doing my best to keep myself invisible. The whispers from my classmates have started again now that Kellan hasn't been by my side. They've collectively decided that he was only with me because he was trying to fuck me. I can't exactly say they were wrong, considering that's exactly what happened. We fucked, and he left.

I just can't let myself believe it was a lie. He has to have genuine feelings for me. It felt like he loved me, even though he never said it. He made me feel special for the first time since my grandmother passed away.

The doubts have started creeping into the dark corners of my mind and as much as I don't want to believe them, there's nothing to stop them without him here. The nagging urges that I've always felt are scratching at my seams, begging me to let them free. *How could I think he loved me? How could anyone even like someone like me? I'm nothing.*

"She called him her boyfriend. How pathetic. She's still not over Carson," I hear someone say as I walk past.

Fucking Carson had to go and run his mouth to make this even worse. He went and told everyone about how I came home with some random guy, called him my boyfriend, and then asked if I wanted him to watch me fuck the guy. He has everyone out here thinking I'm some psycho ex, hellbent on revenge because I saw him fucking Lexi. I just want him to leave me alone. The end of this school year can't come soon enough.

I have nobody now, completely secluded like a true outcast from society. This is how I've felt my entire life. I've never been good enough, and every time I finally think things are going to change, they go right back to the way they were before.

It seems so ordinary to continue on at Thorn Grove as though I haven't been introduced to Death himself. I let myself have feelings for him, dare I say love. Tossing a word like that around is dangerous and I haven't known him for long, but I can't control the way I feel. The connection we have is like nothing I've ever felt in my entire life. It's intense and confusing.

"What a dirty skank. I can't believe she still has the gall to show her face on campus," someone says as I walk past.

"Do you think she let him film her too?" another person says as I ignore them and turn the corner. I run straight into Carson and the bitch who called me a slut in the dining hall after the video got sent out.

This is the last thing I needed today. I'm sure they're about to make me feel smaller than I already feel. It's like Carson lives to torment me. He can't help but be a massive douchebag.

"Hey, Lena. Where's your new boyfriend?" he says, and I can hear the sarcasm rolling off his tongue.

"Fuck off, Carson." I try to step around them, but he steps in front of me, stopping me.

The girl he's with eyes me up and down as if she's trying to find something to ridicule me for. She's so full of herself, thinking that she's God's gift to mankind, but in reality, she's just another insecure mean girl. It's not like we have any kind of shortage of those going around.

"You are such a nasty skank. I can't believe you wanted Carson to watch you fuck someone. As if he has any desire to be anywhere near your dirty cunt again. You're really into some weird shit," the girl says.

I look her dead in the eyes, not letting her words bother me. "Do you enjoy being his flavor of the day? He was fucking Lexi, too. You're not special."

"You realize I was fucking him while he was with you. What makes you think I give a shit about having him to myself? I know he will come back to my bed because I'm not a whore like you." The girl laughs.

"How are your arms doing, Lena? Do you have any new scars? Did you think about me when you did them?" Carson laughs. "If I told you I was fucking other people for our entire relationship, would you go back to the apartment and cry about it? Maybe cut yourself again?"

I stare at him in disbelief. I don't even know how to respond without completely breaking down. I thought I was strong enough to not let his words hurt me, but I don't think I am. Maybe if Kellan were still here for me to confide in, it would be different.

He looks over at the girl standing next to him. "Did you know her parents practically begged me to date her? How fucking pathetic. They wanted to make sure their damaged daughter ended up with a decent man instead of killing herself."

"She should do everyone a favor and just do it already," the girl says.

"Wouldn't be a loss if you ask me," Carson says.

Fuck all of them and everything they have to say. Tears well up in my eyes, but I refuse to let him see my weakness. "Good thing nobody asked you," I spit, trying to stay strong.

I turn on my heels, not wanting to hear another word from anyone on this campus and march directly to the parking lot where I parked my car. I need to get the fuck out of here. I'm giving myself the rest of the day off again.

After a few minutes, I'm driving down the road. Now that I'm away from the prying eyes of everyone, I can let it all crash in on me. I don't have to pretend anymore, and I can't stop it from happening. Tears soak my face, blurring my vision.

I'm nobody. I'm worthless. Nobody wants me. I should just kill myself. That's what they all want. What the hell am I even doing with my life? Why am I never good enough for anyone? I wish Kellan were here to take this feeling away. Being around him would calm me instantly but he doesn't care. I tell myself even though I know it's not true. My chest heaves from the rush of emotions. It's all too much, and I don't want to feel any of it. I want to turn it off and go numb, but I can't.

The gates of the cemetery appear, and I want nothing more than to be on my blanket with the dead. The dead don't make me feel bad about myself. They don't judge. They don't make comments about something my shitty ex-boyfriend did that I had no control over.

I slam the car in park and open the trunk to grab the blanket but glance over to the supply of razors and bandages in the bag next to it. The last time I used them was the day Kellan found me and comforted me. He made me feel safe. He made me feel like, for the first time, I didn't need the release from the cool metal gliding across my skin.

I reach down and grab the package. Slowly, I pull out a shiny blade and hold it up. I stare at it for a moment, debating whether or not I need the release. I can feel the anxiety eating at the depths of my soul. The darkness inside me begs to be freed so she can make everything better again.

Without a second thought, I drag the metal across my skin and lose myself in the feeling of the scraping along my wrist. Blood drips down from the cut. It's deep this time, but I doubt it will be deep enough to kill me. *Would that be so bad, though?*

The blood stops dripping from the cut after a few minutes, and I stare at the mess I've made on the grass behind my car. I still feel too much, and I want to be numb, so I dig into my arm again and watch as the blood begins to flow freely. Over and over, I repeat the process but never cut deep enough. The cuts actually seem to be getting more shallow as I go. It's like there's a part of me holding back.

I'm tired and I can't keep feeling like this. Mentally, I'm back to where I was two years ago on the bathroom floor at my parents' house. The weight of the world is too much, and I'm suffocating. *They told me to kill myself, so what's stopping me?*

I take a deep breath, and the scent of fresh rain surrounds me. The familiar, clean smell causes my heart to swell. *Is he here? Is Kellan watching? If he is, then why hasn't he shown himself to me? Does he want me to just get it over with, like everyone else?*

If I die, maybe I'll get to see him again, but would it be longer than a brief moment? I hold the blade up to my wrist, willing myself to make the final cut to end it all. I'm torn on what to do. I sit here and stare at my wrists and the blood covering them from the other cuts. Why am I hesitating this time?

Chapter 15

Kellan

It's pure fucking torture having to stay away from her. I can't show myself, but I've never left her alone for longer than I have to. I leave to reap souls and immediately pop back up in the shadows wherever she is, following her around like a lost puppy.

She was strong for a few days, but all of that is gone. It breaks down every part of my being, knowing that I am causing her pain. I want to appear, pull her into my grasp, and never let her go. I want to tell her she is perfect and how much I love her, but I am forbidden until her purpose has been fulfilled.

Hearing the things people have been saying to her is gut-wrenching, and Carson is the worst of all of them. I hope that when the time comes, wherever his soul ends up, it is tortured for eternity.

It took every ounce of my self-control to not appear in front of them when that vile girl told my pet to kill herself. I want to take her pain for her, but I can't. It's all for her purpose, but knowing that doesn't make it any easier. She needs to be strong.

If at any point I feel like she can't get through this on her own, I will say fuck the rules and show up to stop her before she ends it all. Regardless of what The Others want, I won't let her go through with that.

I have to believe she will get through this and that the connection we've established can withstand whatever she feels right now. I can sense she is on the fence about how I feel.

I want to shake her and tell her she's wrong. I am wholly in love with her. She consumes my entire being and is the start and end of all of my thoughts. As soon as I can show myself to her again, I will make sure to tell her every chance I get. I should have told her before, when she saw my true form and accepted me. She didn't stray away and not telling her was the stupidest thing I've ever done.

Another soul calls out for me to lead them, but I can't leave my girl yet. She is running to her car, and I want to ensure she's okay. She seems so hurt. Soon enough, she will never have to experience sadness like this ever again.

The pain of dealing with their existence will be over because she will be fully mine. I will never let another soul harm her again. She will only endure what she chooses, and everything else will be nonexistent.

I appear in the cemetery to wait for her to pull in. When she gets here, she immediately goes to open her trunk. I want to wipe the tears from her face. I thought she was grabbing the blanket she likes to lay on, but she didn't grab it. Something else caught her eye first. I feel the call for another soul who needs guidance, but again, I ignore it. I won't leave her—not like this. Something is going to happen. I can feel the shift in her emotions.

I watch as she grabs the blade and brings it down on her wrist. She cuts herself over and over again to try and escape her feelings. She is overwhelmed with everything and nothing all at the same time.

It's torture to let her go through this, knowing that if I appeared, I could hold her until she was okay and calm all of her thoughts. I have a peaceful effect on her because her soul knows it belongs to me. She has always belonged to me, even if neither of us were aware of it yet.

Time passes, and I inch closer and closer to her. I can't risk showing myself, but I still want to be near her. I stand only a few inches away now, but she is none the wiser.

She looks between her wrist and then to the blade for a moment before her nostrils flare. She smells something in the air, and her eyes shoot up to glance around but she's disappointed when she sees nothing except the empty graveyard around her.

Her eyes seem so defeated, lost, and confused. My perfect pet, all alone. Soon, you will never be alone again. You will be by my side every single day until the end of time. We will never be away from one another unless you will it.

Something shifts in her demeanor, and I can tell this is the moment everything has been leading up to. Anxiety fills every fiber of my being to the pits of my shadows.

She is toying with the idea of living or dying. She is right back to feeling the same things she felt when I first crossed paths with her, and I feel guilty that she has to feel like this again. That awful yet glorious moment when I laid my eyes on her for the first time.

This moment will change our entire future. She will decide whether or not she will succumb to the pressures of life and end it all. Her purpose will be decided in mere moments and it's too much for me to handle. Allowing her to feel so low might be the hardest thing I've ever had to do.

I move away, in fear of stopping her before she can make her choice. I can't do anything right now besides pace from a distance, silently willing her to choose me, us. I will intervene if I must, but fuck, I hope she can do this. *Come on, pet. Make the right choice. Stick it out for me, please.* The Others testing her like this is inhumane and part of me will always resent them for it. I just hope she can forgive me for allowing this to happen.

Chapter 16

Lena

I've never had a reason to hesitate when it comes to self-harm. I've always wished for death with open arms, but this time, there is someone else I have to consider. Someone who may actually miss me. That same someone also happens to be Death himself.

I guess I still wish for it but in a different way now.

My parents think I'm a burden. My mother is only worried about how bad I make her look. My father is only interested in how I can benefit his business. They still don't know I ended things with Carson. Don't even get me started on that bag of shit. I let myself believe he was a good companion, and I was so fucking stupid.

I'm stuck on what to do. *Just kill yourself; nobody will care.* The thoughts spiral in my mind, but I can't make myself go through with them. Something is holding me back. I can smell him all around me, but he won't show himself. Is he testing me? Am I imagining it in hopes of him showing up?

"Kellan?" I cry out, but there is no reply. "Now would be a good time to show up if you're going to. I'm so fucking lost, and I really need you. I just want everything to stop. I want the hurt to go away. I want you," I tell the empty air around me, and still, he doesn't show himself. "You told me you would try to come if I called. Where are you?"

Tears stream down my face, and my chest heaves up and down. I wipe the snot from my nose with my non-bloody arm and continue to stare between the blade and the spot on my wrist where my radial artery could so easily help me bleed out.

Thoughts swirl inside my head. Life has done nothing but beat me down. *Do I want to end the pain and be free? Yes.* I can't do it, though. I won't do it. I can't leave this world without making sure Kellan knows exactly what he means to me. He needs to know how he's changed me.

Life. I think to myself, and a new peaceful sensation fills me. I fell for him. I love him. Should someone's purpose be determined by a man or a personification of a man, in Kellan's case? No. But by love and life, maybe. Love is the one thing that every being naturally seeks. We want to give it and receive it, and you are never alone when there is love.

I was at a crossroads, completely torn with what to do, until now. For the first time, everything is clear, and I drop the blade. My arms fall to my sides, and I choose to live.

I don't know what will come from the students at Thorn Grove, my parents, or anything else that has been plaguing me. For the first time in a long time, I want to actually try to push through my dark impulses.

If things aren't working here, I will go somewhere else. I will forge the life I deserve for myself. I will struggle, I know that, but this newfound peace that surges through me has me believing I can do anything.

My tears dry up, and I look up toward the sky. I feel free from my thoughts and confident in my decision. I take another deep breath and steady myself, smelling the air around me as crows caw out in the distance.

It feels like someone is watching me, and I turn to see a figure appear directly behind me. I'm frozen in place, unsure of whether or not my eyes are playing tricks on me. A shadowy form with green eyes stares back at me with smokey tendrils reaching out toward me. It's as if they are yearning to touch me again.

"Pet?" he questions, and I burst into tears.

All of my emotions crash down on me at once. Any doubt I felt over his feelings for me fades away the moment he's back in my presence. I throw my arms around his neck and pull him into me. He shifts into his human form, and his lips land firmly on mine. Our tongues dance for dominance before he bites down on my lip, making me moan.

I missed the feel of him on me, the way his energy surrounds me with nothing but everything all at the same time. Electricity pulses to my core as he slides his hands down my back and grips each one of my ass cheeks, making me moan in his mouth. He lifts me up, and my legs wrap around his waist before he inches us backward to place my ass on the edge of my car's trunk, and his hands come up to cup my face tenderly. I feel his hard cock pressing up against my center, and I lean into it, shamelessly grinding myself on him.

He groans, and his mouth leaves mine. "I missed you so fucking much. It's been torture being away from you."

He leans in and presses his lips against my neck, and I tilt it to the side to give him better access. One of his hands moves toward the back of my head, and he tangles his fingers in my hair, jerking my head further to the side.

I slide my arm down his back and wince at the pain from the fresh cuts along my wrist. I glance over at them and notice I've started bleeding again. To prevent blood from getting all over him, I push him back. Confused, he stands in front of me, and I shamefully pull my arm close to my chest.

He looks down at my wrist and frowns. "You never need to be ashamed of this. I've told you before."

Instead of reprimanding me about using cutting as a coping mechanism, he leans around me to grab something from the trunk. He holds out his hand, indicating for me to give him my arm, and reluctantly, I do.

In addition to my bag of clothes, I've started keeping a small first aid kit, fully stocked with a bottle of peroxide. He takes the lid off the bottle and pours it over the cuts, making me hiss at the stinging sensation. Tiny bubbles flicker through the wounds as the liquid does its job, cleaning away any bacteria. He leans in to blow it dry once the pain subsides and the bubbles settle. The feel of his gentle breath on my skin gives me the chills. He grabs a large gauze pad next, carefully placing it over the cuts and taping it in place. It's not the best bandage, but it will do.

I jump down from the edge of the trunk, suddenly feeling a bit too vulnerable to continue our little make-out session. He eyes me wearily before stepping toward the trunk to pull out the blanket and looks at me with a mischievous smile.

"Stay," is all he says as he walks toward the gravestones I usually sit near.

"What am I? A dog?" I call out, but I do as I'm told, staying right in place.

I lose sight of him as he steps behind the large bush, blocking the view of my favorite bench. After a few minutes, I grow impatient and walk around the bush to find him. I see him hovering over my blanket, placed in the exact spot we first met. His shadow form beckons me to come closer, but he shakes his head.

We should talk about everything that transpired over the last six days, but all I want right now is him. I want to be consumed by him and worry about the rest later. He hovers there as though he is waiting for me to make up my mind. I want him to make me feel good, happy, and free from the darkness.

"Kellan," I breathe out, and he groans in approval.

"Crawl to me, pet. Crawl through the sea of the dead to get to your master."

His words shoot right to my core, making my pussy weep, and I want to obey more than anything. Am I really about to crawl through a graveyard?

One of his shadowy tendrils extends out just far enough to wrap around my neck in a leash-like fashion and pulls me toward the ground, making my decision for me. My knees collide with the soft dirt, and my pussy flutters from the forced position. My eyes lock on his familiar greens, and slowly, I crawl toward the one thing I've wanted more than anything, Death.

His tendril stays firmly wrapped around my neck, guiding me. With every inch forward, I find myself growing wetter and wetter. My fingers tangle in the overgrown grass, and I make sure to arch my back so he can see my ass sway with every movement.

When I finally reach the blanket, I stop before him, leaning back on my heels. I place my hands on top of my thighs in a submissive position and keep my eyes trained on the ground, but a tendril reaches out to tilt my head up.

"Such an obedient slut for me."

His words send shivers down my body. I am his slut. Only his. If anyone else were to say something like that to me, it would be triggering, but coming from him, I know that he says it from a place of warmth and love. He knows I love being degraded and is all too willing to make that happen for me.

Without another word, the shadow around my neck frees itself as several other tendrils shoot from him. They rip off every piece of clothing I'm wearing and toss them to the side before retracting back into him. My nipples instantly harden in the cool air, and I shudder as it hits the rest of my bare body. I ache for him to touch me.

"Get back on all fours, pet. I want to see how wet your pussy is for me."

Immediately, I lean forward, placing my hands on the blanket, and spread my knees a little wider than necessary to proudly display the soaking wet mess between my thighs. He glides behind me with the feathery touch of his shadow hand sliding from my shoulder, down my back, and over my ass.

Something trails up my inner thigh, and the anticipation of his touch overwhelms me. Inch by inch, my breathing picks up, and my heart slams in my chest. I try my best not to squirm, but I've never wanted someone as badly as I want him right now.

Finally, a featherlight touch slides across my dripping center, making me moan. My back arches, begging for more, and I hear a deep chuckle behind me. I turn my head to see that Kellan has partially shifted into his human form.

He kneels behind me, his cock so close yet still so far away from my pussy and brings a palm down to slap my bare ass.

"I've missed being inside this sweet cunt," he says, and before I can react, two fingers are shoved inside me. "You're like a drug I can never get enough of."

He pumps them in and out at a quickened pace, curling them in the perfect position to make me moan in pure bliss. It's like he's on a mission to make me come as fast as possible. It won't take long. I can attest to that.

"Kellan," I pant. "Please."

"I love when you beg like a greedy whore."

"More," I say.

He pulls his fingers out of me and shoves his cock in their place with one brutal thrust.

"YES!" I cry out at the intrusion.

He grips the sides of my hips tight enough to make me wince, but all I can focus on is the way his cock fills me. He pumps in and out of me so perfectly. I slide my hand down to rub my clit but am shocked when something that feels like a whip slaps my ass.

His hands are still holding my hips, but when I look over my shoulder, I see a shadow tendril floating just above my backside. I glance up at Kellan with hooded eyes, and the tendril smacks down on my cheek again, sending electricity through my body.

His body is a mixed morph of shadow and human, with some parts of him being more defined than others. A sly grin crosses his face, and he whips my ass again. My pussy clenches, and I throw my head back to relish in the mixture of pleasure and pain. A cool shadow rubs over what is likely a raised red welt to soothe the sting.

"Fuck, your pussy is gripping me so tight. Are you going to come for me, pet?" he asks before releasing a hand from one of my hips and gripping the back of my neck.

He pushes my head down until my face meets the blanket. From this position, he can slam into me harder and faster than before. A faint touch glides over my clit, rubbing circles and working me right to the edge of pure gratification.

"Look at my pretty little slut getting fucked in a graveyard by Death himself."

A new pressure finds my clit, almost as though his shadows are pinching it, and I see stars. Tingles spread throughout my body, and my eyes roll back in my head. My fingers clutch onto the blanket, and I let out a loud moan.

"Come for me. Be a good fucking girl and drench my cock."

"Kellan!" I scream as my body obeys his command, and I come for him. His pace never slows as I ride out the intense orgasm. My toes curl inward, and my pussy convulses. For a moment, it feels like it's never going to end.

Once my body finally levels out, his hand leaves the back of my neck, and I feel him lean down to whisper in my ear. "My perfect girl, you've changed everything in the best possible way."

I feel something fill me as he groans behind me. He finally slows his thrusts and pulls out of me, shifting fully into his human form. We fall onto the blanket next to one another and I pant on the ground, trying to catch my breath. Clarity finally comes back to me, and I look over to find him staring directly at me. He's always looking at me as if I am the only thing that exists to him.

"Where were you? It's been almost a week. I tried calling out to you, but you never came." I bite my lip, nervously awaiting his reply.

"They told me I had to stay away." His face is stern, and he seems visibly distressed by the admission.

"They?"

"Yes, The Others." He sighs and runs his fingers through his hair. "There's a lot I need to catch you up on."

"I've got nothing but time." It's the truth. I don't plan on going back to Thorn Grove any time soon. I can't bear the chance of running into Carson again. "Do you have to leave again?"

"No, pet. I'm never leaving you again. As long as you want me by your side, I will be there." He places a finger under my chin and leans in to kiss me again. His soft lips have me practically melting in his hand.

"What about your work? Don't you have to leave to reap the souls?" I don't understand how he says he will be by my side at all times if he has a job to do. I won't keep him from that. It's entirely too important.

"I do, but you can come with me instead of staying here."

My brow furrows. I don't understand. Go with him? How the hell would I do that? He can travel in shadow form. He literally appears and disappears on command. Surely, if that were something I was capable of, I would know it.

"I can sense the thoughts racing through your mind. Give me a moment. I'll explain everything." He seems tense even though moments ago, we were just relaxed. It's almost as if whatever he's about to say is more difficult than it should be.

I nod and brace myself for whatever he has to tell me.

Chapter 17

Kellan

As soon as she chose to drop the blade, I knew her purpose had been fulfilled. She chose to live. The Others didn't need to tell me because I could sense the change in the air. I can always tell when the souls in my realm complete their purpose.

I appeared in front of her as soon as her decision was made because I wasn't wasting another moment without having her in my grasp. She seemed shocked to see me, but I could tell she was also relieved. She could have chosen to end it all, and I could have lost her forever. The demon would have tried to take her, but she chose life. She gave us a chance forever, even if she doesn't know it yet.

There is still so much she needs to know. Now that her purpose has been fulfilled, I am free to tell her. If she is going to stay here in my realm, she will need to have full knowledge of everything. No more secrets. It will be out on the table, and my only hope is that she will still look at me the way she is right now after she finds out the truth.

"Stay here. Let me go grab you some clothes so we can talk," I tell her and vanish, only to reappear at the trunk of her car.

I grab a pair of black leggings, lace panties, a bralette, and a long-sleeve red sweater with stars on it.

When I get back, I hand her the clothes and wait for her to dress. I materialize a pair of black jeans and a hoodie for myself. One of the more convenient things about having the magic I do is that I can clothe my human form in whatever I want with the snap of my fingers. I take a seat on the bench next to the blanket, and once she is fully dressed, she comes over to sit next to me.

"Pet, there is something you need to know." I reach out to caress the side of her face with my palm.

Her eyes fill with worry. Her entire human life was plagued with people disappointing her. After some reflection, I've realized it was part of her journey here in my realm for people to test her in order to see if she would succumb to the same temptations she did before I brought her here.

"I have never in my entire existence felt for a soul the way that I feel for you. I've never loved anything before you, and I will never love anything other than you. You changed everything, Lena."

"Kellan," she whispers, eyes filling up with tears.

"I love you, Lena Hill. I love you so much that it consumes me. I feel whole when I'm with you. There was a part of me that I never even realized was missing until I saw you. You complete me."

The sides of her mouth tip up slowly, and a huge grin spreads across her face. She goes to say something, but I reach out my hand to hush her. I know what she's about to say, and I don't want her to regret it.

"Before you say what you're thinking right now, I need to tell you everything. You need to know what you are walking into here."

"Okay." Her brows furrow and she opens her mouth to say something else but snaps it shut, waiting for me to continue.

"Two years and five weeks ago in your time, I laid eyes on you for the first time to reap your soul. You were lying in a puddle of blood, and you looked so weak, barely hanging onto your human life. Your mother rushed in to try and save you, but she was unsuccessful."

I hear a sharp gasp as her eyes widen. She is piecing together everything she knows about me and why she can see me now.

"You have been a soul in my realm, on your path to fulfill your purpose since the first moment I saw you. I carried you here and placed you in the hospital that you woke up in after the incident. Everything you have experienced since that bathroom floor has all led up to today when you fulfilled your purpose."

"You're going to have to pause here for a damn minute because I have some questions."

"I will answer any questions you have."

"Has this all been fake? Carson, Lexi, Thorn Grove? It's all made up?"

"No, they are also souls on their own individual journeys to fulfill their purpose. Every interaction you had with them was genuine. Everyone here is a human soul, aside from me. The

Others make the rules regarding purpose, but it is my understanding that certain souls are meant to cross paths and interact with one another as tests. It is how they separate the pure souls from the impure ones."

"But nobody knows they're dead? Nobody is old? Why are there so many others going to a fake college?" she questions.

"It would be hard to test the purity of a soul if they knew they were dead and being tested, would it not?"

"I guess."

"Once I leave the soul on their path in my realm, all memories of their death are forgotten. In my realm, their age is based on what is required to fulfill their purpose. Most of the time, humans experience major growth and development between the ages of 18 and 30. It's why that age is so common here."

I push a stray piece of her hair behind her ear, and she leans into the touch. Good. I haven't scared her away. I was worried this would be too much for her.

"Once a purpose is fulfilled, the angel or demon appears to take the soul from here. They are the official representatives of each, good and evil. God and the Devil are in command, but their angel and demon both have access to my realm."

"Balance," she says.

"Yes. As far as the college goes, this is not the only area of my realm. This is just one corner. There are other towns, islands, forests, boats, you name it, and it's an available option here."

"Kellan..." she trails off, and I think this is it. This is when she decides it's all too much for her.

"Yes?"

"You're telling me there's an endless number of places for me to live, and I've been living with my ex-douchebag at a college where everyone bullies me? Why did you let me stay there?"

I reach out and hold her hand in mine. "I couldn't reveal this to you and risk The Others taking you from me. I know that was selfish of me, and I'm so sorry, pet. I intended to show you my true form and figure out the rest, but that plan went to shit when I appeared in your bathroom, and you realized it was me."

"That's your fault! You could have appeared outside the apartment door or something."

"Hmmm. I suppose I could have," I admit.

Her body visibly tenses. "Anyway, back to Carson. Please tell me I don't have to go back there. Tell me I can stay with you now, that I don't ever have to see any of those people from Thorn Grove again."

"You do not have to see any of them again. We can go wherever you like. If you'd like to stay near this cemetery, that can be arranged. Or we could curate a place together that we can call our home. Wherever or whatever you decide, I will be by your side." I've never sounded so hopeful in my entire existence. I never desired a home for myself, but a home for us sounds perfect.

She breathes out a sigh of relief, the tension leaving her body. "How long do people usually stay here?"

"It varies. It could be a matter of moments, years, or decades. There is no real sense of time here, only the illusion of it. Time ends when a soul's life ends. How long someone is here directly relates to fulfilling their purpose."

She sits on those words for a moment before her eyes meet mine. "How long have I really been here? It feels like it's been two years and five weeks, but is that how long it's really been?"

"There is no appropriate answer to that question. What I can tell you is that every moment of not being with you was pure torture."

"What do you mean?" She seems a bit thrown off.

"I told you before, I was drawn to you from the moment I first laid eyes on you. I wasn't joking. I had to bring you here and watch from a distance for so long. Time works differently for me. As I've already said, there is no start or end. The only reason I even came out of the shadows when I did was by accident. I was terrified of messing with your path. I thought if I did, The Others would take you from here sooner. I got a little too close to you the day we met here, and well, you know how that day ended."

She smiles briefly at the memory of the day before her face falls flat. "What happens to souls once they fulfill their purpose and leave here?"

"That I do not fully know. They are taken to a place where I have never been and will never go."

Her body tenses up, and immediately, I am worried all over again. Fuck. All of her emotions are so intense they terrify me. She has me spiraling around, wondering just what she is thinking.

"What is it?"

"I'm dead," she finally says out loud. "I fucking did it. I killed myself, but I still came here and felt completely worthless." Tears fill her eyes, and I pull her into me to comfort her.

"I know it's a lot to take in. Take your time."

"Does that mean they will take me now? You said I fulfilled my purpose, and that's why you were able to show yourself to me again. Will I ever see you again?" Tears spill from her beautiful eyes and her chest heaves.

I can tell she is starting to panic. I try my best to soothe her, but she's become inconsolable. Snot covers my hoodie, so I push back on her shoulders, forcing her to look at me. I hold her in place, staring down at her as two shadowy tendrils extend from me to wipe her tears away.

"You are mine, Lena. Nobody will ever take you from me. Do you understand?" I look at her with nothing but fierce determination. "I would eradicate the entire Cosmos before allowing someone to take you from me. The only way you will ever leave my side is if it is your choice."

That seems to stop her sobs completely. Again, my smoky extensions wipe her face clean from the snot and tears before dissipating back into the air.

"I don't think I'll ever get used to that."

"What?"

"The fact that you can morph between a shadow and a human so easily. It's warm and cool at the same time."

"Do you not like it? I can be in whichever form you prefer."

"I want you to be you. It doesn't matter to me what form you are in. Whatever makes you the most comfortable. Besides, both forms have their benefits." She grins devilishly.

"Please tell me you wish to stay with me. I would never force you, but I don't know what I will do if you decide you want to leave."

Her hand reaches out to cup my face in the most tender way. I've never been someone's sole desire, but when I look at her, I can sense that I am. I still need to ask her the questions, though. I never want her to think she doesn't have a choice in any of this. I won't spend eternity with someone who feels trapped.

"I think my soul recognized you. I've always belonged to you, and I'll always be yours, just as you have always belonged to me, and you will always be mine," she tells me, her eyes shimmering with admiration and vulnerability.

"You're right about that, pet." I lean in and kiss her, letting our tongues twist along one another.

She tastes so sweet. I could lose myself in her until the end of time. Another soul calls out to me in the recesses of my mind. They need reaping, but they will have to wait. There is no way I'm leaving my girl right now. I pull her under my arm, and we sit like that for a while in silence, enjoying each other's company. I know she has more questions, and I will answer them all whenever she asks.

Chapter 18

Lena

I fell in love with Death, both literally and figuratively. It may be completely insane, but I can't help it. He makes me want to be a better person, not only for him but also for myself.

"Kellan, I know you said they won't take me from you, but how is that possible? If everyone else is taken away, why would they leave me?" I ask, terrified of how he is going to respond. My hands tremble slightly, so I tuck them between my thighs.

"When you saw me in my true form and recognized me, it broke one of their rules. Nobody is to see me in my true form unless they are being ushered to my realm after their death. I was forced into a conversation with the representatives The Others sent."

"The angel and demon?" I ask.

"Yes. These were strange circumstances. I am always to remain neutral, yet here I am, in love with a human soul. I was going to tell you everything that night, but you put the pieces together yourself." He smiles at me adoringly, and it pulls at the strings of my heart. "Your brilliant mind. You are the reason they gave us a chance. Technically, I did not break the rules. I did not reveal myself, and you were still unaware that you were a soul in my realm. Because of this, they decided you could have one more opportunity to fulfill your purpose. They were very firm in that I could not intervene this time. It had to be all you, because if I involved myself in any way, they would have taken you from me. It was agony watching you suffer, but I had to give us a chance. I believed wholeheartedly that you would have the strength." He shakes his head as though he is ashamed of himself for leaving me to deal with the brutality of Carson and all of the other students at Thorn Grove.

"Do you know what my purpose was?" I whisper.

This is such a simple question with an immense meaning. The entire time I've been here with Kellan has led up to this one moment, and I desperately want to know what that was.

He seems so secure with his answer. "I believe it was life."

"Life?" I mimic.

"Yes. Strange as that may seem, I was able to deduce your purpose the moment you dropped the blade in the trunk of your car. You chose to live rather than end it all. It seems every challenge you've faced here was leading you to the moment where you felt the most similar to when you took your own life in the bathroom."

"That's pretty fucking cruel," I state plainly. What kind of fucked afterlife is this, where I'm expected to go back to the point of wanting to kill myself?

"It is, and I'm truly sorry. I didn't know that's what they intended. I never want to see you broken like that again. It hurts me to see you hurt."

"What does all of this mean now?" I ask.

Them pushing me over and over again to get to the point where I wanted to kill myself is extremely fucked up. I already lived through it once, but they felt like I needed to go through it twice. What would have happened if I decided not to drop the blade?

"I would have stopped you," Kellan states like he can read my mind. I already know he can't, but he must be reading my body language.

"They said you couldn't intervene."

"I know. I would have disobeyed them if it came to that. Thankfully, it was never a factor. You're much stronger now than you were when you first came here."

"You're right about that. Everything is different now. Knowing you and what it's like to feel love again has changed my entire outlook."

"You never have to go another day without me, pet."

"Good, because I'm not planning on it. You're going to end up getting sick of me at some point. You realize that, right?"

"Never," he says, pulling me on top of his lap to straddle him.

He leans forward, trailing his nose up my neck before placing a light kiss on it. I whimper as he continues his path up my neck and over to my ear to whisper in it.

"I could spend an eternity with you, inside you, and it still wouldn't be enough."

Goosebumps spread down my arms, and pleasure shoots directly to my core. Hearing him tell me how much he wants me is the hottest fucking thing in the entire world. I grind my pussy on him, and his hands reach around to grab my ass, aiding me in the process. He's hard, and I find myself craving his cock again.

I want to please him more than anything, so I slide off his lap and onto my knees between his legs. I look up and pause, silently asking for permission, and see the glint in his eyes. My hand reaches up to the button of his pants, and I slowly unbutton them before sliding the zipper down. He doesn't make any sort of effort to try and stop me or assist as my hand reaches inside to free his cock. He eyes me intently, waiting for my next move as I look down at his raging hard-on to see the tip of it leaking precum. I lean in, lock my eyes on his, and reach out my tongue to lick the tip.

"Fucking perfect." He groans. A smile forms along the edge of my lips.

Very slowly, I take him into my mouth, swirling my tongue along the way and listening to the pleasurable sounds he makes. I take my time sucking, bobbing my head up and down, all while working my tongue. My hand grips the base of his shaft, pumping it in tandem.

"Always so greedy for my cock. The perfect little whore for me."

His fingers tangle in my hair, and all of a sudden, he takes complete control, shoving my face to his pelvis. I choke, struggling to breathe as his cock cuts off my airway. His body begins to morph into a mixture of shadow and human as he thrusts his hips into my mouth.

Tears well up in my eyes as I try my best to keep my throat relaxed and let him use me. Fuck, I love when he uses me. A cool shadowy tendril wraps around my throat, further cutting off my ability to breathe as he brutally thrusts into my mouth.

"You're the perfect slut for me, aren't you, pet?"

I grumble yes around his cock because I am his slut. I will gladly be a slut for him until the end of time. I've moved my hands to his upper thighs, holding on for dear life as he fucks my face for his pleasure. What I don't expect is to feel pressure between my legs. One of his shadows found its way to my clit and is firmly rubbing it from the outside of my leggings.

Tears stream down my face, and drool has begun to drip from my chin as Kellan continues to thrust his cock in and out of my mouth. Darkness begins to fill the corners of my vision. There are so many feelings all at once. The shadow finds its way inside my leggings and directly to my pussy to shove itself inside.

"Look at you choking on my cock with tears streaming down your face. You better not waste a drop when I come in this pretty mouth. Take it all like the greedy pet you are."

The pressure on my throat releases, and the shadow inside me pushes and pulls, rubbing my walls in the perfect place. I find myself right on the edge of a climax as his cock jerks against my tongue, and I feel the spurts of his come shooting into my mouth, making me see stars.

My pussy flutters around the tendril, and an all-consuming pleasure shoots through my body. I buck my hips and moan, riding out the intense pleasure. This orgasm is less intense than the one earlier but still just as satisfying. He pulls his cock from my mouth, and a string with a mixture of drool and semen drips from it.

A whooshing sound fills the air behind us, and I turn to look at what caused it. I am stunned to see two figures standing next to the blanket behind us. My cheeks heat, likely turning a scarlet red from the embarrassing act of being caught in such a salacious position with Death.

Kellan chuckles and tucks himself back into his pants. His shadow leaves my leggings while his hand reaches out to wipe the dripping mixture of drool and come from my chin. He caresses my cheek afterward, reassuring me that he is right here with me.

His focus goes to the two figures standing behind us as he shifts back into his true form to address them. I move from my kneeling position to stand next to him. I'm not sure why they are here or what this means for our future, but I know he will protect me.

"Angel, demon, sorry if you saw anything inappropriate. Me and my girl were just... reuniting." He snickers as the angel rolls their eyes.

The demon actually laughs at his prodding toward the angel, and I let my body relax a little with their playful banter. Surely, if they were here with bad news, they wouldn't be joking around—at least, I hope not.

"We don't intend to stay here long, reaper. We just came to settle things with your human soul," the demon says.

My body tenses, and I look up at Kellan. He senses my worry, and his shadows pull me into an embrace as the conversation continues.

The angel looks over at me, demanding my attention. "You have completed your purpose. If you were any other soul, you would be leaving this realm with me. I take it that it is not something you are interested in doing?"

"No," I state. There's no sense in sugar-coating it. I won't be leaving with anyone besides Kellan.

"Very well. You have been given the option to stay in this realm with the reaper if you'd like. This choice cannot be undone. You will be Death's responsibility for all of eternity."

Death's responsibility. Like that's something he has to be burdened with. I look over to the source of everything I love and find him staring down at me with nothing less than pure admiration.

"Are you sure you want me forever?" I ask, giving myself one last moment of doubt.

He leans in and wraps his shadowy tendril around my throat to pull me closer to him. "If you doubt my feelings for you, pet, I may have to punish you for it."

Fuck me. Everything inside me melts, and I glance up at him adoringly. "Do you promise?" I grin, not knowing what's gotten into me. I just can't get enough of him.

I look back over to the angel and demon. "I'm staying with Kellan."

"There is one more thing you need to know. You will no longer be a human soul should you stay here. As you know, human souls are not meant to be in this realm permanently. Your essence will be transformed into a being similar to the reaper, a shadow being with the magic to appear in either shadow or human form. You will become an assistant to Death, his companion. As he is responsible for you, you will be responsible for aiding him with the reaping of human souls."

My brow furrows. I'll be a shadow being, too? I didn't anticipate that, but I suppose it's better than never seeing him again. Will he still want me when I'm more like him?

"You're okay with all of this?" I ask him.

"Lena, this choice is yours and yours alone. I never want to live a day without you. I've told you this already. I love you more than anything."

"I love you too," I tell him, shifting my attention back over to the two intruders in our realm. "I'm staying."

They nod, and the demon steps forward to snap his fingers. My body lifts into the air, and tingles overtake me. It's a weird sensation. I feel cold and nothing at the same time. My human emotions are still there, but the overwhelming feeling of despair and worthlessness that I've always felt when I'm not around Kellan is gone. I'm becoming the version of myself that I was always meant to be.

Magic continues to work through my body until, finally, it stops. I float just above the soil in the graveyard, my body billowing around me. I pull my thoughts together and bring my shadowy form to a shape that resembles a hand and hold it in front of my face. Oh my fuck, I'm a reaper. I look over to Kellan again, and he eyes me intently.

"Do you still want me like this?"

"I'll always want you," he says before leaning in to place a chaste kiss on my, um, I guess my face. I don't really know. I'm still trying to get this shadowy blob under control.

I take a breath and center my thoughts. Finally, my body transforms back into my human form, and my feet are planted on the ground. I look down at my clothes and see the outfit that I was thinking about covering my body. Never having to buy clothes will be a nice perk.

The angel and demon exchange a look between the two of them and then back over to Kellan and me. It seems a bit like they are wondering if I'm going to bail out at the last minute, but I'm all in.

"We are done here then," the angel states, but that's not good enough for me. After everything I went through, they don't get to just show up and then leave without answering any of my questions.

"Wait," I call out, and they both turn to look at me. "What about Carson?"

"I took Carson from this realm after he told you to kill yourself," the demon grins. "He's been having quite a good time where I dropped him off, don't you worry."

"So, he's in Hell?" I ask

"Something like that," The demon says with an evil smirk, neither confirming nor denying.

I should feel bad Carson is likely going to spend all of eternity being tortured, but I don't give a flying fuck. He deserves it for all the shit that he put me through, for all the humiliation and shame I had to feel because of him. I know now it was all for a reason, but that doesn't make it any easier.

He took every opportunity he could to make me feel bad about who I am. He rubbed it in my face that my parents wanted him to date me out of sympathy. Wait. My parents aren't here. They were never here if I died on that bathroom floor.

I turn towards Kellan. "My parents didn't tell him to date me?"

"He believes they did, but no, they didn't."

"How is that possible?" I ask.

"This world mimics the human world. Any interaction that is not face to face, or with a soul who is currently inhabiting this place, is simulated. In your case, this would apply to the text messages you had with your parents, and Dani. Their responses to your messages were based on how they acted in your human life. Sometimes, this is a way people are tested. Dani was a test for you. It was to see if you had the strength to walk away from her, and you did. Your parents were a test for Carson. When he threw it in your face, it was further proof of the kind of person he was to his core."

I take a deep breath, letting myself be okay with the fact that Carson was exactly the soul he made himself out to be. I look over toward the demon. He is waiting for me to finish with whatever questions I have so he can go back to wherever he resides.

"Make him suffer," I say, my eyebrows narrow as the words leave my lips.

"I can send you a message every now and then to prove he's being carefully taken care of if you want."

A sinister grin crosses my face. "I definitely want that."

"If you ever get bored with her, send her my way. I see why you're so infatuated," the demon says to Kellan.

"You'd do well to stay the fuck away from my girl," Kellan grits and the demon holds his hands up in defense.

"I suppose we should be leaving now. I wish you two nothing but the best," the angel says, and with that, the two of them vanish into thin air, leaving Kellan and me alone in the cemetery again.

He looks over at me with the purest love in his eyes. "Are you ready for our forever?"

"Forever," I say as I shift back into my shadow form.

Epilogue
Kellan - Sometime later

I'm not sure how long it's been since Lena made the choice to stay by my side. Time doesn't have a start or finish in our realm, but every single moment has been nothing short of a gift. No amount of time with her will ever be enough.

She is my beginning and ending, my entire reason for existence. The two of us have grown closer than before as we've begun exploring the change from her being a human soul to a shadow being like myself.

At first, she was worried it might affect the way we feel for one another. She wasn't sure if I would still care for her in the same capacity I did for her human soul, but my feelings for her have only continued to intensify with each passing moment. It's partially due to her actions. She is so gentle and kind.

Today, she held an old woman's hand as we walked her into our realm. Seeing how completely selfless Lena is makes me so much more thankful for her. She cared for that old woman with nothing but the purest intentions.

Most days, I struggle between whether love or lust will overtake me. I can't resist her. Ever since she chose to stay, it's as though our shadows can't get enough of one another. The electric feeling that encompasses us when we touch is unlike anything. It's fucking intoxicating. We find ourselves entangled in one another any chance we get, like two halves to one whole, and I will never complain about it.

All of the souls who were complicit in bullying her when she was at Thorn Grove have moved on from our realm. Aside from Carson, she was there to watch as the demon took each and every one of them. They deserve it after what they put my girl through.

I've been trying my best to experience everything she enjoyed during her time as a human, and she has been eager to show me. Just yesterday, I conjured a waterfall for us to visit. We had a picnic lunch and sat at the base of the rocks. The feeling of the cool mist from the water splashing against our shadows was my second favorite part of the day. My favorite was when she came all over my cock in the water.

Most of our time is spent in our shadow forms. With every passing moment, she becomes closer to who she was always meant to be. Without the hardships from her human life, she is thriving.

Today, I have something extra special planned for her. I saw a familiar name pop up on my list, and I'm going to surprise her with the honor of being the one to reap this particular soul. It's a name she's mentioned to me before while speaking of her past. It's a person who played a significant role in her choice to end her human life. Ross. The piece of shit who her best friend chose over her. He cut her hair and bullied her to the point where she felt like being dead was a greater relief than life itself.

She hasn't felt the need to self-harm since she became my equal. I make a point for her to always know how loved and cared for she is. If she ever felt worthless or unwanted, it would be solely my fault, and I will never let that happen.

She appears in front of me, not wasting a moment before wrapping her arms around me. I pull her back and look down into those deep brown eyes that I love so much. I give her a chaste kiss, and she peers back at me with a furrowed brow.

"I would love to fuck that greedy cunt until you can't walk, but we have somewhere we need to be. I have a surprise for you."

"Oooooh, I love surprises! What is it?" Her shadows spiral from her, fueled with pure joy, and I have to do my best to keep my composure. She's so fucking perfect.

"A fun name popped up on my list not too long ago. I think you're really going to love this one."

Her eyes go wide with anticipation. She isn't a murderous being, but she does get a sense of satisfaction from being the one to help certain souls cross. We've taken several people who bullied her in high school, and they all freaked out when they saw her. She laughed about it for an abnormally long period of time. I will do anything to hear my girl laugh or make her happy.

"Who is it this time?" she inquires.

"It's Ross," I state and watch her shadow morph into a human form, wearing the cutest white sundress with dark purple tulips. Her hair has grown out a bit and falls just above her breasts now.

It has the most beautiful natural wave to it. I morph back into my human form and smile down at her.

"You better not be lying," she states.

"I would never lie to you. You know this. He is all yours to reap if you want him."

"Of course I want that son of a bitch. I can't wait to see the look on his dumbass face when I show up as my shadow self and then transform into my human self right before his eyes. It should terrify the shit out of him. Fucker deserves so much worse, but I'll take what I can get."

He deserves to burn in hell for the things he did to her. It doesn't matter what kind of atonement he made throughout the rest of his life. Sometimes, there are things and ways you affect people that you just can't make amends for. With any luck, he will be in and out of our realm in no time.

"We can go whenever you're ready. His name is at the very top of the list."

She wraps her arms around my neck, pulling me close. Instantly my cock strains in my pants, longing to be inside her. She raises up on her tiptoes to bring her soft lips to mine, and I lose myself in her, taking every little bit she is willing to give. When she finally pulls back, she smiles.

"When we get back, I am going to take care of that." She drops her arms from my neck and takes a step back, casually grazing one of her hands along the outline of my cock.

Before I have a chance to respond, she transforms back to her shadow form and dissipates from my line of sight. I shake my head and follow suit, already knowing where she is going.

We appear in an old one-story house that has maybe a total of four rooms and is extremely dilapidated. The roof has several small tarps being held down by large stones. I don't know how they haven't fallen. The house is a complete shit hole, but it doesn't matter; we're not here for a hotel stay. We're going to get this son of a bitch and get our asses back to the cemetery so I can drive my cock into her aching cunt.

I glance over at her, and she disappears again, so I follow. When I appear next, we are inside the home, planted right in the living room. There's a couch and an old coffee table with drugs sprawled out across the entirety of it, but not much else. This fucker's demise is front and center for us to see. The spoon and lighter are still sitting on the table. We stand there for a moment, looking at his dead body before his soul reveals itself to us.

"Who the fuck are you?" he spits.

"Your end," Lena tells him, and I can tell she is going to remember this moment forever.

"My end?" he questions, turning to see his dead body on the couch. "What the fuck? I'm dead?"

"You sure as fuck are you slimy piece of shit. We are here to reap your soul and lead you to your purpose. With any luck, you will find it quickly, and the demon will take you to where you truly belong," Lena spits, her tone flat and vicious.

"I'm not going anywhere with the two of you."

"You're right. You're not going anywhere with the two of us, but you are going with me," Lena says as she shifts to her human form in front of him.

I'm pretty sure her actions are frowned upon by The Others, but they haven't told us to stop, so we have no intention of doing so. There are only a few people left who tormented her in her human life, and the ones we cross paths with will all forget about this moment once they enter our realm anyway. This is all for her to heal.

She takes a step toward him in her white and yellow sundress with purple tulips. His eyes widen with shock as he tries to figure out if this is some sort of fucked up dream.

"Remember me, asshole?" she says, and he stumbles backward.

"Lena Hill? It's not possible you're-"

"Dead," she cuts him off. "Yeah, just like you. Welcome to the afterlife. You get me as your friendly guide."

"How the hell is this even possible?"

"You see, once Dani decided she was going to cut contact with me for your loser ass, I killed myself. Then I fucked Death, and, well, here I am. While you go on to be tortured for all of eternity, because let's be honest, we all know that's where you will end up. I will be right here thinking about how satisfying this very moment was."

"Fuck you, dumb bitch."

I step forward, and one of my shadowy tendrils grabs his neck, squeezing tightly. He may only be a spirit, but his soul still feels everything a human soul does.

"Watch how you fucking speak to my girl."

She looks over at me with sparkling eyes, nodding for me to release him. Reluctantly, I do as I'm told because this is her moment. She takes a step closer to him and shifts back into her shadow form, deciding he has seen enough of her human one. She wants to show him she has evolved into someone stronger.

"You will come with us to fulfill your purpose, and I will be watching you. You won't know it, but I will be right there when the demon comes to take your soul."

One of her shadow tendrils reaches out to grab him by the throat, and without another word, we disappear to our realm to bring him to his purpose. We appear in a run-down shopping center. His time here won't be much different than the worthless life he was living as a human. The two of us bring him over to a picnic table beside the building and drop him there with replicas of the spoon and lighter that were on his coffee table. He will think he got a little too high and passed out.

Lena looks over at me, satisfaction crossing her face, and with that, she disappears again. I follow her, not knowing where we are going to end up, but when I appear in the cemetery, I can't help but smile.

I wander over to her favorite bench, only to find her naked and spread out for me on top of a small blanket in her human form. She's sitting back on her elbows with her knees bent and her legs parted.

"Fuck me, Kellan. Don't make me wait."

"How can I resist my greedy girl asking me to fuck her?"

My eyes drop to her already soaking cunt as her fingers tease her clit. So fucking perfect for me in every single way. I close the distance between us, shifting back into my human form. We always start out this way and then morph into a mixture of solid and shadow where the beginning and end seem to blur.

I drop to my knees between her legs and lean forward, laying on my stomach to place my face right in front of her pussy. I wrap my arms around her thighs, pulling her closer to me, and pepper kisses up her legs. Her back arches, and she lets out the sweetest whimper, willing me to touch her more.

My tongue reaches out, and I lick up the length of her once, twice, three times before her fingers tangle in my hair, and she pulls me closer, smashing my nose against her most sensitive area. My mouth latches around it, sucking and flicking her clit.

"Kellan," she moans.

Fuck, I love the way my name falls so easily from her lips. If I heard it every second of every day, it still wouldn't be enough. I pick up my pace, licking her, and slowly slide two fingers into her dripping pussy. She's always so wet for me. When I begin moving them in and out, she pushes her hips up in response and whimpers.

"Greedy little slut, aren't you?"

"Yes," she admits, making my cock jerk below me. "I'm so close."

"Beg me, pet. Beg me to make this pretty pussy weep for me."

"Please, Kellan," she cries out as my fingers continue to slowly thrust in and out of her.

I look up to see raised eyebrows and nothing but pure pleasure plastered all over her face, so I give her what she wants. I curl my fingers inside her, hitting the perfect spot that makes her see stars every time. Her pussy squeezes my fingers, and I know she's close. I keep a steady rhythm, focusing my tongue on her clit, my fingers curling into that spot over and over with the steady momentum of them thrusting in and out of her.

"I'm coming!" she screams and pulses around my fingers.

Her mouth makes the perfect 'O' shape, and her eyes roll back. Seeing her come undone is a drug I'll always be addicted to.

"Such a dirty slut coming all over my fingers." I pull them out and creep my body up hers before shoving my fingers into her mouth. "Taste how sweet you are."

She doesn't even hesitate to swirl her tongue around them. This fucking girl doesn't even know the power she has. My form begins to partially shift, sending pure electricity through every fiber of my being. I look down to see her in a similar form.

Smokey tendrils emit from the two of us battling with one another for dominance. I wrap a tendril around her throat, and she wraps one around mine. Another one of hers reaches out to guide my shadow cock to her center.

"I need to feel you inside me."

I roll onto my back next to her and pull her on top of me to straddle me. She looks down, smiling as my hands reach up to fondle each of her breasts before my fingers roll her nipples between them. She grinds down on my cock with approval. There is so much happening at the same time between the two of us now that each of our shadow forms seem to have their own agendas.

She lifts herself up and slowly lowers her pussy onto my very hard and ready cock. Smoke emits from us, blurring the lines from where the two of us begin and end. We are one. She begins to circle her hips, using me for her every need.

"Ride my cock like a desperate whore. Take what you need and make both of us come, pet."

She moves her hips slowly at first, enjoying the feeling of my hard length filling her up before she begins thrusting forward and backward in a quick motion. I grip onto her shadow form, aiding her thrust and shoving myself deeper inside her.

"Always so fucking tight," I grunt as her hands land on my chest.

Our tendrils finally free themselves from each other's throats, and she digs her nails into my chest, leaving a trail of red lines in their wake. We both begin to feel the building lust between our bodies, and she makes the sweetest sounds. The whimpers. The moans. She is nothing short of perfection through it all.

"Kellan," she cries as I thrust harder, hitting that perfect spot. She throws her head back and loses all sense of control.

"Let me feel that pussy strangle my cock."

She grips down on me, and it's all I need to find my own blissful high with her. She comes apart around me as I shoot my release inside her. We keep a steady pace until both of us come down from our high. When I pull out, my come drips from her pussy, and a shadowy tendril sweeps over to push it right back in.

We default fully to our human forms and pant for air. It's the perfect time of day when the sun begins to set, and the sky has started to shine hues of pink and yellow. I pull her up to a seated position and tuck her under my arm on the blanket, loving the way she feels next to me. Her naked body with mine. The two of us mold together so perfectly. She looks up and smiles.

"We have to get some work in soon," she says. "There are souls ready for us to reap."

"Let's just stay here for now. They can wait a little bit longer. I want to watch the sunset with my girl."

She reaches up to stroke the side of my face with her hand. "I love you, Kellan. I will always love you. Death is my life. You are my life."

Hearing her confess this makes me even more grateful for her—this one previously human soul who changed the course of everything for both of us. My equal.

"My beautiful girl," I say, admiring her. "My love for you is endless, the kind of love that doesn't exist in time and space. It's a love that has no beginning and no end. It just is—now and forever."

"It's you and me to the end, isn't it?" she asks me, her eyes glinting with joy.

"You and me for eternity, pet."

I lean down and kiss the tip of her nose, holding her close as the sun sets on the horizon. Everything is how it was always meant to be: me and the girl who was always destined for me in my arms and bringing light to my darkness. I couldn't ask for a better way to spend every day until the end of time.

Acknowledgements

First and foremost, thank you to my readers. You are changing my life in ways I can't even begin to explain every time you take a chance on one of my books. I love you all beyond words!

This book was hard for me to write. Some of the thoughts and feelings are raw, personal experiences. Being someone who struggles with mental health and existing in the world isn't always easy. I found healing in Lena, and I hope you did as well. If you struggle, just know you are not alone. My messages are always open. Tomorrow is a new day no matter how hard today was.

Hubby, you are my number one supporter and I'll always be forever grateful for you! I love you more than words can express.

Sarah, Mickie, and Jessica, my alpha babes. Thank you so much for being there to answer all my random questions about shadow peens. You three are irreplaceable.

To my beta team, you are the best group of ladies an author could ever ask for. Thank you for all the time you invest in not only me but my books. I love you all so much!

Taylor, thank you for squeezing this one in and being the best editor out there! Having you alongside my entire journey as an author has been so rewarding. You're an amazing human and I appreciate you so much!

About the author

K.M. Baker is a Dark Romance author who lives in a small town in Pennsylvania with her husband. She has three dogs, two German Shepherds and a Bichon Frise, who are like children to her.

Writing has always been a dream, but she never had the courage to do it until recently.

Most of her free time is spent reading all the spicy books she can get her hands on (the dirtier, the better). Outside of reading, she enjoys gardening, crafting, and taking her 1972 Sprint Mustang to car shows. Coffee, red wine, and blankets are some of her favorite things to indulge in. She is passionate about traveling and hopes to one day move and live outside the US.

Stalk Me:

Tik Tok: @K.M.Bakerauthor

Instagram: @K.M.Bakerauthor

Facebook: K.M. Baker's Bookworms

Email: KMBakerauthor@gmail.com

Also by K.M. Baker

The Darkness Duet:

Evading Darkness

Darkness Falls

Standalones:

The Afterthought

Endless